BITTER TRAIL

Lazy Jake Fontell and his partner Buffalo Bob have gone into the freighting business. Approaching El Paso, they have no idea of the troubles they will encounter after coming to the aid of a dying Mexican. Before succumbing to his injuries, the grandee gives the pair a map detailing the location of an icon that was worn by the legendary Aztec leader Montezuma. A secret revolutionary group has sworn to overthrow the Mexican government — and he who wields the headdress wields the power . . .

DALE GRAHAM

BITTER TRAIL

Complete and Unabridged

LINFORD
Leicester

First published in Great Britain in 2014 by
Robert Hale Limited
London

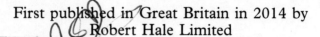

First Linford Edition
published 2015
by arrangement with
Robert Hale Limited
London

A catalogue record for this book is available
from the British Library.

ISBN 978–1–4448–2608–1

Published by
F. A. Thorpe (Publishing)
Anstey, Leicestershire

Set by Words & Graphics Ltd.
Anstey, Leicestershire
Printed and bound in Great Britain by
T. J. International Ltd., Padstow, Cornwall

This book is printed on acid-free paper

1

Everything Goes in Witchita!

The wagon drew to a halt on the edge of the dusty border town. Deep ruts in the desert sand indicated that it was heavily loaded.

Lazy Jake Fontelle removed his broad-brimmed Texas high crown, releasing a mass of dark brown hair. The unruly thatch was in need of professional care. Not to mention the nose-twitching smell emanating from a sweating torso. That was no surprise as he and his partner had been on the trail for the last three weeks. Displaying a marked degree of casualness as befitted his nickname, the wagon boss dragged a grubby bandanna across his brow.

A hot noonday sun beat down from the cloudless sky as dust devils swirled and cavorted in a frenetic dance around the wagon.

'Been a long trip,' remarked Jake's partner. Buffalo Bob slotted the long bull whip into its holder. 'Was beginning to think we'd never get here.' The old skinner uncorked a water bottle and took a long slug. His gnarled features twisted into furrows of disgust as he spat out the tepid liquid. 'I can hardly wait to knock back a proper drink now we've finally arrived.'

This was the first time that either man had visited El Paso.

The old hunter was avidly studying the wide main street ahead. Names such as The Gem, Big Muddy and Randy Rooster brought a smirking glint to his narrowed gaze. And likely there were more of the same further down towards the riverbank. Saloons to be sampled once their consignment had been delivered and they had been paid off.

'Keep your eyes peeled for Longbow's Mercantile,' Fontelle reminded his partner after noting that well-known gleam. 'We still have plenty of work to do before hitting the town.'

Gathering up the reins, Bob pressed the team of six back into motion.

The town had a rip-roaring reputation. It was situated on the banks of the mighty Rio Grande. Occupying the far shore was the Mexican dive of Paso del Norte. Even at this time of day when the sun was at its zenith, the main street was teeming with a mixture of whites and the instantly recognizable Mexicans. Their swarthy complexion and dress code instantly marked them out.

And there was another reason.

A recent town ordnance decreed that those visitors from south of the border were barred from the wearing of firearms. The greasers had been blamed for trouble caused by an excessive consumption of hard liquor. As a result, there was little love lost between the two factions.

By 1877, El Paso was by far the more prosperous of the two settlements. The town had gravitated into an important crossing point into Mexico and in consequence had become a major trading centre for the exchange of goods.

Fontelle Freightline intended to capitalize on this affluence. They were carrying a host of factory-made items unavailable south of the border. Jake was as eager to unload as his grizzled associate. A veteran of the war, Jaylord Fontelle had been a major in command of the Third Kentucky Rifle Brigade.

Bob Cantrell was his trusty and reliable sergeant, who had stayed on with the army as a civilian buffalo hunter following the cessation of hostilities in 1865.

The two army colleagues had lost touch until the previous year. They had met up by accident in Witchita, where Bob had taken a job as doorman for Mattie Silks. She was the well-endowed madam who ran the town's leading house of ill-repute.

It was a meeting that was to have

violent consequences.

Two drunken cowpokes had tried to muscle their way into the whorehouse without paying. Their notion was that an aging dude like Buffalo Bob was easy meat.

How wrong they were.

'Where do you think you're going, fella?' the ex-skinner rapped out as the beefier of the two pushed past him.

The war veteran didn't wait for an answer. He grabbed the heavyset jasper by the scruff of the neck and slung him back into the street. Before his buddy had a chance to react, a solid right hook to the jaw found the guy joining his sidekick. The pair scrabbled about in the dust trying to shake the mush from their addled heads, unsure what exactly had occurred.

A brusque warning enlightened them.

'And don't come back here again unless you want more of the same.' Bob stood on the boardwalk, legs apart as he stared hard at the two wastrels. His right hand rested on the heavy truncheon slung around his waist. 'Only men and paying customers are welcome in the Red Garter.'

Pecos Pete Sinclair growled out a threatening rejoinder as he scrambled to his feet.

'You made a big mistake, old man,' snarled the burly cowpuncher, 'going up against Flying V drovers.'

Sinclair grabbed for his revolver. As he thumbed back the hammer, his finger tightened on the trigger. It was all ready to haul off when a cutting interjection stayed his hand.

'Ease back on that trigger if'n you want to remain standing.'

The cowpoke's gaze shifted to a tall, loose-limbed guy who had just emerged from an adjacent alley. The soused ruffian was looking straight down the barrel of a Winchester carbine, which was aimed at his chest. The face of the man holding the repeater was cloaked in shadow. But a piercing red glint in the guy's chilling regard proved that he meant business.

'Watch out, Pecos!' his sidekick

cautioned. 'Don't do anything stupid.'

But the warning from Red Sumner had come too late.

Sinclair's stultified brain took no heed of his partner's alarm to step back from the brink; nor indeed the cold yet cogent threat from the intruder. His gun swung towards the intruder.

A man of few words, Jake Fontelle wasted no more on the reckless braggart. The die had been cast. Flame and death spat from his Winchester. A duo of lethal slugs punched a hole in the cowpoke's chest, spinning him around like a performing seal at a freak show. Arms waving, he tumbled to the ground.

Smoke dribbled from the carbine's barrel as the lethal piece of hardware panned across to cover Red Sumner.

'Your move, carrot top,' came the nerve-jangling challenge. It was accompanied by the ominous rattle of a fresh cartridge being levered into the barrel.

Sumner had no wish to follow his buddy into the welcoming embrace of the scythe man. His arms lifted in surrender. Frightened eyes stared at the spreading pool of blood now oozing from his partner's fatal wounds.

'Don't shoot!' the cowboy croaked as he backed away. 'This ain't my call. I'm going.'

Fontelle's piercing gaze never left the retreating figure until it had disappeared into an alleyway two blocks down.

Buffalo Bob let out a heavy sigh of relief. 'That was a close call, Major,' he said acknowledging the other man's rank. This was the first time they had set eyes on each other since the regiment was disbanded two years before. 'Those boys were all set to ventilate my hide.'

'Then it's a darned good job I moseyed along at the right moment,' replied Jake with an easy grin. 'That makes us quits after you saved me from an early grave at Chancellorville.'

Bob shrugged. 'You would have done the same for me, Major.'

Fontelle acknowledged the compliment with a brisk nod.

'I ain't no officer these days, Bob,' the tall man replied while thumbing fresh shells into the carbine's loading slot. 'Plain Jake Fontelle will do fine. Or if'n you've a mind, some folks call me Lazy.'

Bob's leathery features cracked into a smile of understanding. It was followed by a hearty guffaw. 'I gotta admit that the way you handled those jiggers sure was the style of a cool dude. Guess the big guy figured you for easy prey.'

'That's the kind of ploy that always gives me an edge,' drawled Jake.

'So what are you doing in these parts . . . Lazy?'

'I've gone into the freighting business. Bought me a wagon and a team of six. It's all loaded up and waiting down at the holding yard on Butler Street. I figured on pulling out tomorrow at first light for Santa Fe.' Jake paused to roll up a couple of stogies. He offered one to his old comrade-in-arms. 'Fact is, old buddy, I could do with some help. It's a lot of work for one man to handle.'

'I already got a job,' said Bob with an apologetic shrug of the shoulders. 'And Mattie Silks has been good to me. Took me in when I was down on my luck. I wouldn't want to let her down.'

'Can't pay much though,' countered the freighter. 'And getting threatened every night can't be much fun. Come in with me and there'll be no more need to roll drunks off the sidewalk.' A twirl of blue smoke snaked from between pursed lips. 'And you can be a partner in your own business.'

Bob was impressed by his old officer's standpoint. He nodded slowly, thinking about the offer. 'I have another couple of hours to do here. It'll give me time to think over your offer. How's about we meet up in the Palace Bar? I'll have an answer for you then. And make sure there's a full bottle of Kentucky bourbon on the counter.'

Lazy Jake's gaze rested on the corpse of Pecos Pete Sinclair as he considered the suggestion. A swarm of greedy flies hovered around the fatal wounds. Such sights were not uncommon in the rip-roaring township, where garish signs informed all comers that *Everything Goes in Witchita!*

Somebody would eventually move the body when it began to smell.

'Better make it sooner,' the concerned freighter shot back, having quickly arrived at a disturbing conclusion. 'That guy will likely tell his sidekicks. And I don't want to be around when a dozen Flying V rannigans come looking for revenge.'

A flea-bitten mutt yapped its agreement with the forceful observation.

'Hmmmm! Guess you're right there,' Bob concurred after a moment's hesitation. 'I'll tell Mattie straight away that I'm going into partnership with an old comrade. She'll understand.'

Jake grinned widely. 'You won't regret it.'

A half-hour later the wagon was pulling out of the freight yard on the edge of town. The pair had opted for a less used northerly trail to avoid an unwanted meeting with the expected cowboys, who were camped to the south.

The business had prospered during that year to such an extent that Jake was thinking about buying another wagon and setting up a base of operations in Santa Fe.

The wagon trundled down the middle of El Paso's rutted highway. Eager eyes scanned the numerous establishments lining either side, searching for a sign that read *Longbow's Mercantile*.

'You spot anything, Bob?' enquired Lazy Jake.

'Not on this side, boss.' Even after six months working with his old commanding officer, Buffalo Bob Cantrell still found it hard to accept that they were now on equal terms. 'Maybe we should ask somebody.'

'Good idea,' Jake agreed, drawing the wagon to a halt.

He asked the next passer-by where the freight yard was located. The large bearded man was wearing a leather apron and toting a hammer which indicated to one and all that he was the local blacksmith.

'Five miles out of town on the banks of the river,' a gruff voice laced with a heavy Swedish accent informed them. Eric Bluetooth pointed a jabbing finger along the way the wagon was heading. 'Monkey John reckoned he could save on taxes by setting up beyond the town limits.' The burly jasper pitched out a sarcastic chortle. 'Only trouble is that he now has to employ guards to stop them Paso del Norte greasers from pilfering his stock. The marshal's jurisdiction don't stretch that far.'

The two freighters considered this piece of news with interest.

'That don't bother us none,' replied Bob. 'Just so long as he pays up the full amount we want for our goods.'

'Just watch out for them Mexican thieves.' Bluetooth grinned back revealing his protruding namesake. 'They don't cause trouble in El Paso any more since the marshal passed a law to stop the wearing of guns in public. But that don't apply once they've left town.'

After they'd thanked the helpful blacksmith the freight wagon lumbered onward.

Just beyond the town a narrow raised terrace separated the red sandstone cliffs from the broad sweep of the Rio Grande. Here the river was squeezed into a shallow ravine where a rickety bridge enabled entry into Mexico on the far side.

The wagon stayed on the American shore, where the rough trail meandered around a series of low bluffs. El Paso was soon out of sight. The trail snaked around two more jutting shoulders of rock. Organ pipe cacti reared up beside the well-rutted highway. They were accompanied by yucca and occatillo with mesquite and salt bush the dominant forms of vegetation.

As they approached another slab of fractured rock the sound of gunfire brought the wagon to an abrupt halt. Both men glanced at one another. The fracas was on the far side of a craggy knoll. The deep-throated roar of rifles merged with the sharper crack of pistol shots.

As to its origins, there was no way of knowing unless they investigated. Bob threw another questioning look at his partner as to whether they should get involved. After all, there could be an innocent explanation. Target practice or hunters potting at varmints.

Then a cry of pain made up their minds. That fearful sound was not that of an animal. It was of human origin.

2

A Present for the Future

Without any further hesitation, both men grabbed their rifles and scrambled up the gravelly slope. The din of battle increased measurably as they neared the rim. Edging cautiously towards the crest, they bent low so as not to expose themselves. What he saw down below sent a chilling ripple of anxiety lurching down Jake Fontelle's spine.

A decidedly uneven contest was being played out with the victim likely to be eradicated soon if something was not done.

All of those involved were Mexicans, which was clearly evident from their attire. The victim of the bushwhackers was concealed behind a dead horse. His four antagonists were laying down a lethal bombardment that no man could survive indefinitely. The victim huddled down behind the horse was unable to return fire without exposing himself to the withering blast.

Jake had always deemed himself to be fair-minded. An equal fight and he would have retired, not wishing to get involved. But this was a totally mismatched contest. Jake's natural inclination was to support the underdog. Bob nodded his unspoken agreement.

Closely followed by his partner, Jake was about to sidle round some sheltering boulders to get closer to the action when a movement caught his eye over on the left of the combat zone. An unseen member of the assailants had circled around behind the cowering man with the intention of finishing him off. The killer stood up, fully exposing himself for a better shot.

With no time for a proper aim, Jake jammed the butt of his Winchester into his shoulder and levered off three shots in rapid succession. At least one hit the target. The back-shooter threw up his arms, emitting a piercing yell as he tumbled off the rocky ledge. But not before he had been given time to launch his own devious attack.

The object of the ambush slumped over his horse.

The sudden intervention had alerted the rest of the gang to the fact that they themselves were now under attack. Jake and his sidekick poured down a barrage of fire upon the surprised aggressors.

Caught out by this sudden intrusion, the ambushers returned fire. Bullets zipped back and forth. But the gang were in a weak position, overlooked by their attackers who were concealed in much stronger cover. Odds of four against two disappeared like a puff of smoke with Jake and Bob commanding the high ground. And they took full advantage of their superior position.

'Just like the old days, Major,' yipped Buffalo Bob, levering the breech of his Sharps 'Big Fifty'. The old hunter had always resisted the persuasive chat of gun salesmen urging him to adopt the newer repeaters. The Sharps had never let him down. The gun's reliability and stopping power was second to none. If'n it could drop a buffalo at 1,000 yards, then mere mortals stood no chance against its deadly accuracy. Bob now proceeded to prove his claim.

Jake grinned back. 'Just remember what I used to say . . . make every shot count!'

A howl of triumph burst through Bob's grizzled beard as one of the gang keeled over. With a blur of movement another cartridge was slotted into the breech.

The tables having been well and truly turned, the leader of the ambushers knew that if they remained pinned down here, it would only be a matter of time before they were picked off one by one. He signalled for his remaining men to back off. Bullets continued to pepper all around the craven antagonists as they hustled back to where their mounts were tethered.

A cheer went up from the low ridge

as a final volley dispatched the panicking greasers on their way.

'You bastards ain't no challenge to veterans of the Third Kentucky Rifles,' crowed Bob, jumping around with glee and waving the big rifle in the air.

It was Jake who brought his old buddy back to the stark reality of their situation. A pair of buzzards joined in the celebration, hoping for some easy pickings.

'We'd better check on that dude who was under fire,' he said, scrambling down the back slope. 'He looks in a bad way.'

The man had not moved since being struck down by the back-shooter. Carefully they eased him on to his back. A groan issued from between clenched teeth. At least he was still alive. Jake dribbled some water between the purple lips. It appeared to bring the man round. Eyelids peeled back slowly as he tried to raise himself.

'Not so fast, *compadre*,' Jake whispered, easing the man down. 'You've been shot. Lucky for you it's only a flesh wound.'

After cleaning up the deep cut, he wrapped a bandanna around the man's head. It would serve until they got him proper treatment.

The Mexican winced as a jolt of pain coursed through his lean frame. He was dressed in the style of a grandee rather than a humble peon. Jake poured water over a clean necker and wiped the guy's face. His age was somewhere in the middle years. And the handmade sombrero indicated that he came from a well-heeled family.

So what had those bushwhackers been after? It must have been something mighty serious to warrant a killing on American soil.

'We'll get you back to El Paso,' said Jake. His face remained inscrutable. The injury was not life-threatening but it needed medical attention. 'There must be a doctor in a town that size who can fix you up good as new.'

The man suddenly appeared to rally.

His eyes opened wide. A trembling hand gripped his rescuer's arm. Then he levered himself up on to one elbow.

'Your words are kind, *señor*.' He groaned, the patrician features creasing in pain. 'You are both Americanos?'

The two men nodded.

'By trying to save my life, you put yourselves in grave danger. I am Don Alvarez de Toledo and I ask one favour of you that is vital to the future of my country's government. Will you help?' A choking cough followed as the Mexican struggled to remain conscious.

Jake dribbled more water between the thin lips. He threw a quizzical look towards his partner. The man's request was intriguing although somewhat disturbing. What could be so vital that had led to his being ambushed like this? But they hadn't been given much choice in the matter.

'We'll do what we can, *Señor* Toledo,' he replied, answering for them both. 'If'n it's within our means.'

That was good enough for the don.

He paused. His ragged breathing faltered momentarily before once again recovering. A surprisingly strong hand gripped Jake's arm. 'Then listen carefully to what I have to say,' he wheezed.

He proceeded to explain as briefly as possible the reason why he had been attacked. His words tumbled out quickly in a staccato burst.

It was to be a bizarre revelation.

Don Alvarez had arrived back at the hacienda owned by the Toledo family a day earlier than expected. His meeting with the Socorro territorial governor to discuss the forthcoming campaign for election to the Board of Trade had passed off without opposition. The ranchero was well pleased with the results. All being well, in three weeks' time he would be able to bring all his experience and integrity in the field of commerce to the benefit of the territory.

Much of the discussion had been concerned with a growing problem of corruption in high places. There were those who sought high office for their own avaricious ends. In particular, a secret society known as the Shadows of Montezuma was showing increasing signs of stirring up rebellion among the lower elements of society.

Led by unscrupulous individuals, their aim was to incite the people into rising up and overthrowing the established order. So far, this secret society had achieved only limited success. But their methods were aimed at striking fear into the general populace. This group of dissidents hoped to persuade the gullible masses that a return to the old rule of Aztlan would enable them to seize power.

The original Aztec inhabitants had been brutally overthrown in the name of Christianity. In truth it was so that the white invaders could appropriate all the gold and material wealth they were sure that the indigenous population were hiding. Against the mounted warriors and their firearms, the Aztecs were powerless. That was many centuries before.

The country had moved forward into a more enlightened age. Yet Mexico was still a nation controlled by a rich Catholic minority.

According to the Shadows, now was the time for the impoverished masses to rise up and once again take control of their own destiny.

Don Alvarez and his colleagues were in no doubt that the threat was real. They were well aware of the myth being propagated. Legend had passed down through the ages claiming that the man who wore the revered headdress of the mighty Montezuma would be all-powerful among their followers.

If such a situation were allowed to grow, civil strife would engulf the country. Mexico would be torn apart. Such a state of anarchy must be rooted out and destroyed before it devastated the entire nation.

The ranchero was well satisfied with the meeting in Chihuahua. His mind was concentrated on the impending struggle to persuade hearts and minds that the government had the best interests of the people's welfare at heart, rather than some fanatical power-hungry diehards. He was under no illusions that he would have a tough fight on his hands.

The ageing dignitary was glad to be home. The last vestiges of day lingered over the notched sculpting of the Sacramento Mountains as he neared the hacienda. He had ridden hard to make it back before night finally claimed the land for its own. Tired eyes avidly scanned the adobe buildings that constituted the Toledo *estado*.

Then a frown creased the leathered features of his angular visage. Why were there no lights on? Surely somebody would be at home. And where was his brother? Manuel was meant to be in charge while his elder brother was away.

Don Alvarez was well aware that the two men had not seen eye to eye recently regarding the operation of the hacienda. But his brother should have been here to supervise the extensive work needed at this time of year. He nudged the fine palomino through the open gates into a broad open space that fronted the main living quarters. Still no lights could be seen, nor any movement, which was far more disconcerting. A sense of unease filtered through the grandee's tense frame.

Then his sensitive hearing picked up a strange hum. Straining to locate the mysterious sound, Alvarez calculated that it was coming from the rear of the premises. He dismounted and moved carefully around the outside of the buildings hugging the brown adobe walls.

Soon he was able to ascertain that the sound was a form of chanting. The bizarre rhythm was accompanied by the throbbing beat of drums.

A strange orange glow percolating through the tree cover could just be made out on the far side of a craggy knoll. Curiosity prompted him to clamber across the broken ground and up to the edge of a small wood. Pushing aside the branches, Alvarez sensed the light was building in strength along with the eerie chanting. Yellow spears of a fire flickered in an open glade like spiteful demons capering in wild abandon.

A ripple of fear coursed through the don's lean frame.

Even though common sense urged him to retreat, his legs felt compelled to move forward and investigate. This was his land, and squatters needed to be ejected. An owl hooted in the distance, disturbed by the intrusion into its domain. Brow furrowed, Alvarez moved closer to the glade for a better view.

He crouched behind a bush. From there he could see a group of people gathered in a circle. They were each carrying a flaming brand and dressed in the ceremonial dress of the Aztec hierarchy. In the middle stood their leader. He was clad in a white robe bedecked with peacock feathers and reciting some form of pagan incantation. Arms outstretched, he clutched a large dagger in his right hand.

Covering his face was the mask of an Aztec high priest.

Suddenly the mournful voice reached a stentorian climax. An eerie hush descended over the clearing. Then, almost as an afterthought, the knife plunged into the neck of a tethered sheep. Immediately the bloodthirsty assemblage erupted in a manic frenzy of cheering and dancing around the sacrifice.

Don Alvarez's heart began to race. His whole being froze in stunned horror at what he was witnessing. What sort of diabolical heathen sect had he stumbled upon? His stomach lurched uncontrollably. The priest was draining the animal's blood into cups which were passed around. In no time the clearing was like a scene from Hell.

The elderly grandee slowly stood up, his mind in turmoil.

That was his last thought. His brain erupted. A wave of red mush descended to block out the appalling sight as he tumbled into a bottomless pit of darkness.

Some time later, the mist began to clear. There was no knowing how long he had been unconscious. Although it was still dark, the incessant throbbing inside his head gradually subsided as the endless night faded. He groaned aloud.

'It would appear that our guest has rejoined us.' Deep and resonant like a refined Scotch whisky, the voice continued, 'It is indeed an honour for our group that you have elected to become the first human offering to our overlord, the great Montezuma.'

Don Alvarez struggled to rise. He knew that voice. For a moment he could not place it due to the wretched trauma his mind had suffered. Then it came to him in a sudden rush of understanding. Also flooding his traumatized thoughts was the reason why the hacienda was devoid of staff.

'Manuel, my brother,' he gasped out. 'What is the meaning of this outrage?'

But he already knew the answer. These people must be associated with the infamous Shadows of Montezuma. And his own brother was a leading activist. These gatherings must have being going on for months but on other estancias. Why had he not recognized the signs?

Too late for recriminations now.

Suddenly realizing the grave predicament into which he had unwittingly stumbled, Alvarez tried to rise. But he could not move a muscle. His body was effectively pinioned. He cried out in terror. A dirty rag was stuffed into his mouth choking off any further sound. Not that anybody would hear his cries, seeing that all the staff had been sent elsewhere for the night.

Malevolent eyes, glinting with pure evil, peered down at him. The blood of human sacrifice was far more potent in the fulfilment of their ancient ritual than that of a mere animal. Manuel de Toledo drew himself up to intone the final liturgy of the pagan cult. His arms lifted to the cloudless sky.

'We, the Shadows of Montezuma, do tender this human sacrifice to our revered master. Accept the blood offering as our sign of dedication to furthering your resurrection and the overthrow of the Christian usurpers who have corrupted our dear country.'

Then he turned to address his trembling kinsman. The unworldly experience had numbed Don Alvarez into total submission.

'But first we must prepare a fitting ceremony for such a distinguished addition to our throng.' He turned to one of his acolytes. 'Take this dog and lock him in the wine cellar. There he will have the opportunity to consider the great part he will soon play in resurrecting the long-dormant traditions of our native Aztlan culture.'

Imprisoned in his own home, Don Alvarez de Toledo was given ample time to contemplate the circumstances that had turned his own brother into a fanatical revolutionary. The dark walls of the underground chamber pressed in on the grandee. For some time, his mind refused to accept that such an unimaginable situation had arisen within his own family.

Eventually his head cleared and he was able to think in a more lucid manner.

'How could things have come to this dire state of affairs?' the tethered man muttered to himself. 'What has happened to the brother I once knew and loved?'

Incidents began to form in his troubled mind: events occurring over the last few months that ought to have warned him that things were escalating. Small in themselves, they now assumed far more significance.

But he had ignored all the signs.

Alvarez had always known that his brother was headstrong and stubborn. But for his own kin to descend to such depths was barely credible. The grandee's noble head fell on to his chest in abject despair.

After what seemed like hours, in fact little more than a half hour, the door of the cellar suddenly creaked open. Don Alvarez stiffened. Had his final moments of life arrived? Was he to die in some bizarre ritual in order to further his brother's crazy dreams of revolutionary ferment?

3

Angel of Mercy

A single figure appeared in the doorway and started down the steps. This person remained silent. No such hysterical wailing to the ancient gods as the don had expected. The figure clearly did not want to be discovered. It slipped across the earthen floor and began to sever his bonds.

'Quickly, my brother-in-law, you have little time left before my husband comes to perform his demonic ritual.'

'Serena!' exclaimed the don, struggling to extricate his stiffened arms from the ropes. 'Is it really you? What has happened? I thought the ranchero had been abandoned when I returned from seeing the governor.'

'Quickly, Don Alvarez,' the woman insisted, drawing the older man to his feet. 'There is little time left. You must escape and tell the authorities what is happening here. Take this.' Serena de Toledo pushed a crumpled piece of paper into his hand.

'What is this?' he asked.

'The location of the revered head-dress of Montezuma. You must find and deliver it to the legitimate authorities. Only then can the revolution that is threatening our country be quelled.'

'I do not understand . . . '

'It is a map that I have copied outlining the exact location of that most sacred of Aztec icons. It lies somewhere in the Valley of Trembling Rocks in Central New Mexico,' *Señora* Toledo explained while helping Alvarez towards the open doorway. She gestured impatiently for the startled don to hurry. 'There is no time to explain further. They will be coming soon. And you must be away from here before then or all is lost. A fresh horse is waiting outside. Now hurry!'

The elegant woman he had known

since she married his brother three years before and had loved as a sister urged his stiffened limbs back into motion.

'But what of you, *querida?*' Alvarez asked. Acute anxiety for the woman's safety was evident in his query. 'How will you explain away my escape?'

'Do not be afraid for me, Don Alvarez,' she assured her brother-in-law. 'Manuel thinks that I am staying with my friend Consuela. He has no idea that I know about his insane plans to seize power with the connivance of the naïvely susceptible *campesinos*. That is the reason I came back, knowing you might stumble upon his gory practice. It is as well that, like you, I returned earlier than expected. Now come quickly!' She hustled him out into the forecourt where a saddled horse was waiting.

The grandee took the woman in his arms and thanked her.

'Remember what has to be done,' she firmly reminded him. 'For Mexico. Our country is counting on you.'

Somewhat mesmerized at the rapidity with which this bizarre train of events had escalated, Don Alvarez replied, 'I will do my best to thwart my brother's insane plans. It is a difficult and dangerous task that you have set me, Serena. Let us trust in the Lord that I will be successful.'

He pushed the map inside his jacket, then quickly mounted up.

'*Adios*, and may the saints in Heaven also bless your quest.'

The whispered plea from Serena de Toledo resounded inside his head as he urged the horse into a gallop. Soon he had disappeared into the murky gloom.

A spine-tingling chanting had resumed in the hidden glade as the preparation for his anticipated sacrificial offering to the pagan gods continued. Manuel de Toledo was almost ready for the final countdown to perdition.

Serena knew that she could not remain in this house of infamy for a moment longer.

The wounded Mexican grandee paused in his narration. His breathing was laboured. The noble countenance was waxy and bloodless. It was obvious that the unfolding of his recent ordeal had completely exhausted him. He slumped back gasping out one final request.

'You . . . have saved . . . my life, *señor.*' The words uttered were faltering and slurred. Jake was forced to place an ear to the Mexican's mouth to hear what he was saying. 'I am in no fit state to continue but you can take my place.'

Don Alvarez fumbled inside his coat and removed the map which he handed to his saviour. 'The responsibility of securing my country's future I now place in your hands. Those brigands who have escaped will report back to my brother who cannot be far behind.'

The elderly man's eyes closed but at least he was still alive.

Jake was lost for words. A lump stuck in his throat. To be accorded such a crucial role in a nation's future was beyond his understanding. He was just a humble freighting operator, not some knight in shining armour seeking to find the holy grail like in those stories he'd read as a child. Yet here he was being forced to wear the mantle of a legendary hero.

Buffalo Bob read his thoughts.

'Seems like you've become a modern-day King Arthur and I'm your Merlin,' muttered the old skinner, who had clearly read the same book. 'Only problem is that I ain't one for casting spells.' He guffawed as a notion came into his mind. 'Except when I've had a skinful of rotgut. Then I can do anything.'

Jake gave his partner a reproachful look. The uncanny state of affairs in which they both now found themselves was no laughing matter. But then its absolute weirdness brought a resigned smile to his normally carefree expression. He couldn't help but accept the funny side of their unwanted predicament.

'You're not wrong there, old buddy,' he responded, giving an uneasy shake of the head. 'Reckon we ought to get back to El Paso pronto and figure out how we're going to follow up with this crazy scheme.'

Jake carefully lifted the don on to his back. Then the two partners returned to their wagon. Now that the shock of their deadly encounter had faded, the danger of their situation began to impinge upon Jake's thoughts.

'Keep your eyes peeled for the varmints who escaped,' he ordered his sidekick, whipping up the team. The sooner they reached the safety of the border town the better.

Eventually, and without incident, the isolated post hove into view. Once the injured man was deposited with the local medic, the two freighters headed back for Monkey John's Longbow Freight Yard. They took a different route to avoid any encounter with the bushwhackers.

'What happened to you guys?' asked the hunched figure of Monkey John when he saw their blood-stained appearance.

Jake shrugged his broad shoulders. The two buddies had agreed that no mention of the attack would be disclosed. It would only complicate matters.

'We found a dead guy on the trail,' replied Jake nonchalantly. 'He must have been ambushed and robbed by bandits.'

'So we took him back to El Paso before coming here,' added Bob.

The freight yard owner accepted the comment without question. 'It's been happening a lot lately. Them Mex bastards have been coming across the border by way of the ferry.' He pointed to a sturdy building down near the riverbank. 'I've had to hire a couple of extra guards to watch over the place at night, else they'd strip me down to the bone.'

The San Christobel Mission had been there since the first invasion of the Spanish some three centuries before. It had since attracted a few huts from which peasants sold goods to those waiting to cross the Rio Grande where a ferry terminal had been established. Perhaps that was the reason for Monkey John siting his business here.

Jake eyed the little man. He smiled to himself. Now he could understand how the guy had acquired his moniker. His overlong arms hung down like an ape's as he shambled along. He even sported a prominent hairy jaw.

That said, the trader was no sucker when it came to business.

Bartering to Monkey John was like beaver-trapping to a mountain man. He always obtained the best deal in any negotiations. Nobody got one over on him.

On this occasion, however, he didn't haggle over Jake's price for his goods. Perhaps his mind was elsewhere, such as whether these darned greaser bandits were going to target him next. With their business concluded satisfactorily to all concerned, Jake posed the question that was foremost in his mind.

'Have you got anything for delivery up in Albuquerque?' He puffed hard on a cigar, trying to appear unconcerned. Bob threw him a wary look but remained silent. 'We have some business to conduct up that way. So I figure to make the trip worthwhile.'

Once again, Monkey John accepted the request without any suspicion that other things apart from business had now taken priority in Jake Fontelle's thinking.

'Got me some cases of finest tequila if'n you want them,' he said, stroking his furry chin while working out the cost. 'Just this once, Jake, I'll give you them at rock-bottom cost. They should make a tidy profit up in that neck of the woods.' John sniffed as he considered the proposition. 'Tequila is one of the few things them greasers have gotten right.'

Jake Fontelle didn't need to think about the offer. 'You got a deal,' the freight haulier concurred, offering his hand to seal the contract.

'Just make sure you keep that firewater out the hands of the Navaho,' Monkey John warned. 'Unlike us white eyes, them savages just can't hold their liquor.'

4

Surprise Cargo

The two hauliers only stopped in El Paso long enough for a much-needed bath and to buy some new duds. At the same time they checked on the progress of Don Alvarez. He was doing well but still required a lot of care. Next they visited the office of Sheriff Dave Mather. But the lawman didn't hold out much hope of catching the bushwhackers.

'They'll be back over the border by now,' he huffed. 'But if'n they try anything in my town, the bastards will get a load of buckshot up their asses.' He tapped the stock of his trusty Loomis to emphasize the point.

Jake didn't press the matter. He was more concerned about pushing on to their destination. The lure of hidden booty with such an illustrious heritage was impossible to ignore. He had promised to pass on the Aztec icon. But acquiring an ancient artefact supposedly dripping with precious gems and caked in gold would secure the future of their freighting business.

If they could assist in foiling a revolutionary uprising at the same time, that would be a bonus.

The only item that he had so abruptly inherited was the map detailing the location of the revered icon. It was clearly not the original, having been copied down quickly by the wife of Manuel de Toledo. That must have been before she released her brother-in-law from the wine cellar. But the detail ought to be sufficient for them to follow.

Jake had heard tell about the Valley of the Trembling Rocks but had never been there. It was Bob who provided the background to the disconcerting name.

'Ain't never experienced it myself,'

Bob mused as they proceeded along the main trail north of El Paso. 'But an old buddy of mine called Tub Sundowner once passed through there.'

'What happened?' a fascinated Lazy Jake enquired, noting his partner's wary frown.

'He told me that the ground started shaking beneath his wagon. Rocks came tumbling down off the cliffs on either side of the canyon.'

There was nothing that Buffalo Bob loved better than relating a good story. He stuffed fresh tobacco into his pipe and lit it before continuing. Jake was forced to wait impatiently much to Bob's delight.

'Come on, you old skin-scraper,' Jake pressed. 'What happened?'

'Weeeellll!' Bob drawled out. 'Tub only survived by diving into a cave. The wagon ended up as a pile of matchwood. One of the horses survived enabling him to ride out unscathed once the quake had finished. But it sure scared the marrow out of his bones.

47

Swore that he'd never venture there again.'

Jake sucked in a mouthful of hot air. 'Sounds like a chancy spot to be exploring,' he said. 'Let's trust that the rocks are sleeping on our visit. We might not be as lucky as Tub Sundowner.'

Buffalo shrugged. 'You don't get nowhere unless a few risks are taken.' It was a philosophical outlook that characterized the old-timer's view of life.

The wagon carried on for another half-hour without either man speaking. Each was cocooned in his own thoughts regarding their forthcoming venture.

They had just passed a rocky landmark known as Big Burro when a strange noise came from behind the bench seat where they were perched. It was Bob who picked up on the alien sound.

'Hear that, Jake?' he queried with a frown.

The younger man pricked up his ears. 'Can't say that I did,' he replied.

Bob shrugged. Perhaps his nerves were playing him tricks. But then the same thing happened again. 'Sounded like a cough to me,' he insisted. 'And it's coming from under the tarp.'

'I sure heard it that time,' Jake agreed. He drew the team to a halt. 'Do you reckon we've got us a stowaway on board?'

'Only one way to find out.'

The two men slipped silently off the wagon and crept round to the rear. Jake placed a finger to his lips.

He intended that whoever had hopped a lift was about to receive a nasty surprise. Taking a firm grip of the waterproof cover, he jerked it aside.

And there, lo and behold, squatted their illicit passenger.

The unexpected revelation was as much a shock to the freighters as to the dishevelled creature now exposed. Their unforeseen guest was none other than a woman.

The rough jouncing of the ride beneath a grubby tarp had done nothing for the lady's appearance. Tousled and matted hair hung over her dirt-smeared face. What had once been an expensive buckskin jacket was scuffed and torn. Worst of all, however, was the smell. It arose from a mixture of rancid tallow fat and beaver pelts, which were among the goods sold to Monkey John.

Yet even after taking all this into account, Jake Fontelle could not ignore the beauteous countenance beneath the dirtiness. Olive skin like burnished gold declared her to be a woman of Mexican descent. And nothing could conceal the svelte shape that lurked beneath the woman's shabby buckskin.

Grey eyes swallowed him up even as the woman shrank away in fear.

'It's all right, *señorita*,' he burbled, unable to ignore the woman's mesmeric allure.

'We . . . we . . . ' Jake's mouth flapped open like a landed trout's, unable to formulate any further discourse.

'What my partner is trying to say, miss, is that we ain't gonna hurt you.'

Bob finished off the sentence, trying his best to prevent his nose from twitching. 'But don't you think that the stage-coach would be a sight more comfortable than our old wagon if'n it's a ride you're after? Or is it that you ain't got the readies?'

'No, no, señores,' the woman exclaimed, delving into her jacket.

Instantly both men drew their pistols. Following their recent encounter with the Mexican bandits, they viewed any sudden movement with intense suspicion, even from a woman.

Wide-eyed, the woman launched into a torrent of Spanish, hoping to allay their concern. Eventually she simmered down and resumed her dialogue in English.

'See, I have American dollars to pay for ride.' She pushed a bundle of greenbacks at the two men. 'I could not catch stagecoach because . . . ' Now it was the turn of the Mexican woman to clam up.

The two men waited for her to

continue. She was clearly upset. Tears welled in the limpid pools. That was enough for Jake to find his own voice again and assure her that they did not wish to know her reasons. That was her concern. And if'n she needed a lift, they would willingly give her one, at no charge.

Buffalo threw a caustic look at his smitten partner and huffed. More times than he cared to recall he'd seen how men became putty in the hands of a pretty girl. And here it was happening yet again.

'That is so generous of you, señor,' murmured the woman, her demure regard thoroughly transfixing the hard-nosed ex-soldier. 'And because you are being so kind to a señora, in distress, I will reveal the true nature of the dire situation in which I have found myself.'

Picking up on the woman's use of the marital term of address, Jake's manner of adulation faltered. 'You are married then?' he queried somewhat deflated.

'That is the nature of my problem.'

The woman sighed. 'My name is Serena de Toledo and — '

Before she had chance to recount her story, the two men gasped out loud.

'You are the wife of Manuel de Toledo?' stammered a bemused Jake Fontelle.

Now it was the woman's turn to express surprise. 'You know my husband, then?'

Bob snorted. 'Only by reputation, *Señora* de Toledo. And it ain't a good one.'

Jake interrupted with a warning frown to his incautious partner. 'Pardon my buddy's clumsy mouth. It tends to run away with him at times. But I'm afraid that we do have some bad news for you.'

The two men shuffled their feet uneasily. Heads hung low, they avoided meeting the woman's anxious gaze. She drew away from them, a worried frown on her brow, her lower lip trembling.

'What has happened that you know so much about my business?' The

53

fearful catch in her voice indicated the rapid turn-around of gratitude into fear.

Jake gently assured the woman that they meant her no harm and were indeed on her side. It took some persuasion and cajoling to assure the Mexican *señora* of their sincerity. He delayed the unpleasant tidings by calling a halt, pointing out that it was getting late in the day.

Jake's partner then bustled about building a fire on which he perched a blackened coffee pot.

Over a welcome mug of strong Arbuckles, Serena was informed by the two men of the unfortunate incident that had led to the shooting of her brother-in-law. Jake hastened to reassure her that Don Alvarez was recovering well at the hospital in El Paso. She also learned that they knew all about her husband's resurrection of a secret society called the Shadows of Montezuma.

Jake then removed the map from his jacket. Serena inhaled a sharp intake of breath as he hurried on to assure her that they were committed to seeking out the location of the Aztec icon.

'Don Alvarez passed the map on to us,' Jake informed the woman. 'We promised to seek out the headdress and make sure that it did not fall into the hands of the Shadows.'

Jake was still torn between an avaricious yearning to cash in on the priceless artefact, and the undertaking that now appeared to include this most delectable female. Emotions concerning the lady were rapidly moving to the forefront of his deliberations.

The woman studied her benefactors closely, trying to decide whether they could be trusted to deliver the valuable artefact into her hands. Or were they merely profiteers seeking to exploit this sudden windfall that had come their way?

The old guy seemed like a genuine character.

But what of Jake Fontelle? He certainly was an imposing gringo. And Serena considered herself to be an excellent judge of character. Handsome and honourable were her final conclusions.

'The reason I chose to hide in your wagon was to escape from the clutches of my husband,' she admitted, peeling back a tress of hair to reveal a large bruise on her face. 'This was the result of my arriving home early and discovering his secret. The *canalla* threatened to imprison me in my own home if I breathed a word to the authorities. But he is a fanatic, totally obsessed by the Shadows. I was sure that he meant to kill me once we were alone. That is why I ran away, hoping at some point to catch up with Alvarez and join him in the search for the icon.'

Both men were incensed at this treatment of such a beautiful woman.

'Well, the three of us can hunt it down together now,' Jake assured her.

Having built up the fire to deter any wandering scavengers, Jake offered his bedroll to the woman, electing to make do with a horse blanket for himself.

A lone owl hooted in the distance as they settled down for the night. Tomorrow was soon enough to plan how they were going to find the Aztec icon.

5

Bungled Robbery

Around the same time that Fontelle Freightline was trundling north, events were shaping up on the far side of the Oscura Mountains that would have dire consequences for the three travellers. Another trio was seated close to the front window of the Jack Rabbit saloon in Carrizozo. The New Mexico town was situated on a crossing of trails. As such it had become an important focus for the local ranching community of Lincoln County.

That was the reason why Charlie Moon, known as Crazy Dog, had chosen it for his first foray into bank robbery. The thin-faced villain nursed a glass of beer, his eyes concentrating on the bank across the street. The Dog's stubble-coated features were drawn tight with the strain of waiting. A white scar across his nose, the result of a knife fight, always itched when he got nervous.

For the fourth time since entering the saloon a nervous peeper flicked towards the clock on the wall. Zero hour was just before five in the afternoon, when the bank closed its doors for the day. Five minutes to go. He had chosen that time on a Friday when he expected the vault to be stuffed full of greenbacks.

Opposite Crazy Dog lounged a thin beanpole who was chewing an unlit cigar. He was more laid back. Tincup Turner was a silver prospector who had made and lost a fortune in the Colorado boom town that had given him his nickname. Since then his luck had dried up. Joining up with the Crazy Dog had made life a sight easier than the back-breaking chore of placer mining.

The third member of the gang was a lumbering hulk whose neck appeared to have been swallowed up by his broad shoulders. A few wisps of mousy hair coated the bullet head. Hoss Bowdry was employed more for his brawn than his brain. But he could be relied on to stand firm when things went awry.

The trio had so far only engaged in a bit of cattle rustling before venturing into the business of robbing stores and the odd stagecoach. Moon, however, reckoned that once they had become adept in the more lucrative arena of bank robbery, their reputations would be assured. Not to mention the thickness of their billfolds.

The Dog had always envied the famous outlaws who could boast exploits to match. Gunmen like Sam Bass, Wes Hardin and Jesse James. Once this heist was reported, he also would be moving into the big time. The name of Crazy Dog Moon would be spoken of in the same deferential tones as those other revered idols.

'Time to go, boys,' Moon hissed, pushing back his chair. The others followed. No further words were uttered until they were outside.

Casually, the three men unhitched their mounts and led them across the street. It was Hoss Bowdry's job to look after them and make sure that nobody interfered with the heist being conducted inside the bank.

'Check your weapons,' ordered Moon, scanning the street. Nobody gave the three men a second glance. 'But no shooting unless they give us any trouble,' he warned wagging his revolver. 'The idea is to lift the dough and escape without a hitch. I don't want us having the same fiasco that hit the James gang up in Northfield.'

The raid up in the northern territory of Minnesota had been in all the newspapers as far afield as Colorado, where Moon was operating at the time. Various members of the gang had been wounded, and the authorities had launched a major manhunt to capture the notorious outlaws. Unlike their cousins the Youngers, Jesse and his brother Frank had managed to evade the law and were soon back in the business of robbing trains.

The highpoint of any brigand's lawless career, train jobs were the ultimate aim for Charlie Moon. His dark piercing eyes blazed with rapture at the thought.

Tincup frowned at the boss's wishful fantasies. On numerous occasions, he had listened to Moon babbling on about how he was going to outshine the James boys. Such boasts were usually voiced following a liberal indulgence in hard liquor. Turner did not share the Dog's ambitions, but he was well aware that the gang leader was crazy enough to make the attempt.

When that happened, Tincup Turner intended to be holed up in a different territory. The Carrizozo job was the limit of his aspirations. But the little guy gave no hint of his scepticism as he replied.

'Don't worry, Charlie,' he assured Moon. 'This dump is gonna be a pushover.' Hoss grunted his agreement. Now that they were fully committed, both men were eager to do the business.

The robbers stepped up on to the boardwalk. A quick look either way, then they moved across to the door of the bank.

Tincup peered through the window. He smiled. 'Nobody inside, boss, except the tellers,' he whispered, 'and they're all counting that lovely dough just for us.'

'Then let's go rob us a bank,' breezed the Dog. He indicated for his sidekick to pull up his bandanna. 'Don't want our mugs gracing a Wanted dodger. Ready?'

Tincup nodded. Moon took a deep breath then shouldered his way into the bank. At the same time, he hauled out a sawn-off shotgun from beneath his coat. The deadly weapon was aimed menacingly at the startled tellers behind the partition. Time stood still as the two men behind the counter took in what was happening.

'Don't you galoots try anything

stupid,' bellowed the Dog, emphasizing the point by waving his shotgun around. 'This shooter is loaded and we mean business.' The sneering tone was as much to bolster his confidence as create an atmosphere of intimidation. He succeeded in both counts.

A choked gurgle emerged from the older teller, whose face had turned white with fear. This was the first time Amos Lander had been on the wrong side of a robbery. But the young teller had more grit. Mitch Allison's face hardened.

Tincup instantly recognized the possibility of retaliation.

'Don't try it, mister,' he warned in a low yet threatening murmur. The hammer of his Colt Model P hogleg snapped back. The ominous click echoed around the wooden walls. 'Sam Colt's patent pacifier don't give no second chances.' Much to the weasel's delight, the man wilted under the pressure.

'What is happening in here?'

The stern question came from a

rotund man who had just emerged from his office at the rear. Henry Allison was the bank boss, and Mitch's older brother.

'On your face, fat boy!' snapped Moon at the bemused manager.

Allison stood there, riveted to the spot. This was not the first robbery in which he had been involved. The notorious James gang had robbed the Kansas City bank which had been his first appointment.

'I said on your belly, bird-brain.' Moon's ragged screech was accompanied by a savage jab from the ugly snout of the shotgun. A stifled groan issued from between Allison's fleshy lips as the hard barrel dug into his ribs.

'W-what do you want?' stammered the manager.

'I'll give you one guess. Now, on your face if'n you don't want your guts spread over that wall.'

The trembling man needed no further convincing. He knew to what lengths gangs like this would go to achieve their avaricious ends. He dropped to the floor.

'That's better.' Moon let out a sigh. Things were going according to plan.

He flung two sacks over the counter. 'Right, knucklehead, you fill these up.' The strident bark was aimed at the young teller. 'And remember, notes only. Silver weighs too much.'

'Now you, grey beard,' he rapped at the old teller. Amos Lander was six months from retirement and had every intention of collecting his pension. He nodded, eager to comply. 'Open the safe.'

Lander's willing look fell away. His mouth dropped open.

Moon sensed the old-timer's hesitancy. 'What's the matter?' he growled.

'It can't be opened for another hour,' Lander gabbled out. 'The safe is on a timer.'

Moon's face assumed a purply red tinge of anger. 'Don't give me that!' he raged, his rabid temper threatening to override self-control. 'I said open the safe now if'n you want to save your miserable hide.'

The threat of violence was all too real but Lander knew there was nothing he or any of the others could do. He felt a wetness spreading across his trousers. His weak bladder had surrendered to pure fear. Moon stepped forward and pointed the shotgun at the quaking figure. He chuckled. But the ugly snarl held no humour. 'This guy has gone and pissed himself.'

But Turner was more concerned with the whitening trigger finger clutching the shotgun.

'No boss!' he shouted. 'You promised there would be no shooting.'

'It's true what Mr. Lander has told you,' interposed the manager, trying to maintain his dignity. 'The safe is on a timer and cannot be opened.'

At that precise moment Mitch Allison slid his hand into a drawer. Seeing the robbers becoming flustered, the younger teller sensed that this was his opportunity to gain some much-needed kudos and promotion for foiling the robbery. His hand withdrew, holding a small Colt

Lightning. The gun lifted.

His brother yelled in panic urging him to stop. But the die had been cast.

Charlie Moon may have been related to a mad dog, but his reactions were swift and lethal. Mitchell Allison's Colt went off first. But he was no gunfighter and the panicked shot went wide, smashing an oil lamp.

A maniacal grin broke over Moon's evil face as the teller tried to cock his gun for a second attempt. He never got the chance. The shotgun blasted.

A full load of twelve-gauge buckshot ripped into the man's body.

The force of the double charge punched him back against the wall. Desperately he tried to staunch the rampant flow of blood pouring from the hole in his chest. It was large enough to put your fist inside. Staggering like a drunk, Mitchell Allison lurched away from the wall, took a couple of paces then pitched forward on to his face.

The distraught manager felt his stomach lurch. His mouth filled with bile. Then he threw up on to the floor. A foul odour of urine and vomit filled the room.

Silence hung heavy in the air after the withering blast. Moon stared down at the bloody corpse. A crazed cast came over his sweating face. The smoking gun hung down by his side.

'Y-you've killed him,' croaked Amos Lander, stating the obvious.

'And I'll kill you as well if'n you try to pull the same stunt,' the outlaw blustered while thumbing two fresh cartridges into the breech.

Tincup quickly took the initiative by grabbing the two money sacks and dragging his half-crazed buddy outside, where Bowdry was waiting with the horses.

Pedestrians on both sides of the street had stopped. The noise of gunfire told them that something bad had occurred. Witnessing the two men emerge from the bank at the run, a couple of them drew their pistols.

Hoss Bowdry might have played no

part in the robbery, but he was a stalwart when the chips were down. He let fly with his own revolver, allowing his *compadres* to mount up. The bullets were well placed, driving the bolder citizens back under cover. Turner threw the two loaded sacks up to his buddy.

Hoss slipped the securing loops over the saddle horn while continuing to give covering fire. The fusillade effectively kept heads down, enabling the three robbers to make good their escape.

But the reprieve was only temporary. Irate citizens quickly emerged from cover and began peppering the fleeing outlaws. Laden down with the sacks, Bowdry brought up the rear. His heavy build and the weight of the dough prevented a clean getaway.

Most of the pursuing bullets went wide. But one lucky shot struck his horse in the rump. The animal stumbled and went down. Bowdry threw himself to one side. Quickly recovering, he scrambled back on to his feet and began returning fire.

One against the whole town was long odds. And Hoss was a big target. He didn't stand a chance.

At the outskirts of Carrizozo, Moon threw a glance behind to ensure they had made a clean break. Shock raked his craggy features when he saw that Bowdry had gone down. More important was the loss of all that lovely loot. He drew his horse to a juddering halt.

'Bowdry's been hit,' he yelled at Turner. 'He's a goner but I ain't losing that dough. You go back and snatch it up afore those critters reach him.'

'No chance!' the little weasel rasped, voicing his objection in vigorous terms. 'You want it, then get it yourself. I ain't ready for a boot hill burial yet awhile.'

Crazy Dog snarled. 'If'n you're so yeller, then I'll do the job myself. But don't expect the usual cut when I succeed.'

'Go back there and you won't never get the chance to spend it,' pressed Tincup. 'Let's just cut our losses. Better to run away and live to rob another day.'

More bullets were now being aimed their way. The inflamed citizens of Carrizozo had clearly regained their confidence following the downing of one of the outlaws. One slug singed the left flank of Tincup's paint. The animal reared up on its hind legs, snorting with the acute stab of pain.

'I'm getting outa here,' howled the ex-prospector, without further argument. 'You stay if'n you want to commit suicide.' He swung the sorrel round and dug his spurs in hard. The injury to the horse was not too serious providing treatment could be obtained. It leapt forward, forcing Tincup to cling on tight.

With hot lead buzzing all around, Moon at last realized that his buddy was right. Stay around here, and he was dead meat. He cursed aloud at the howling mob, then galloped off after the fleeing sorrel.

The two failed bank robbers didn't stop until they were certain that pursuit had been evaded. Moon signalled a halt on a low rise that offered ranging views across the bleak terrain in all directions. There was no distant rising cloud of dust to indicate that a posse was in pursuit.

That was little consolation to the Dog, who cursed his bad luck. Their first bank job and it had ended like this. One man dead and the other two chased away like cringing mutts with their tails between their legs in disgrace.

Tincup let his sidekick rant and rave over what might have been. But the misfortune had cleared up one thing for the little guy. He was finished running with Charlie Moon. Hang around with the Crazy Dog and he would surely die in a pauper's grave. Once they reached the next main town, he was cutting loose. But he would keep that notion hushed up for the time being.

6

Pointing the Finger

Once they reached Williamsburg, Lazy Jake Fontelle spent a portion of his profits on equipment deemed necessary for the hazardous expedition to the Valley of Tumbling Rocks. He had found no problem selling the cargo of tequila in the booming township. Being close to Mexico, the fiery tipple was popular with both *hombres blancos* as well as Mexicanos. And there were more than enough saloons willing to pay his price.

As a result they were able to book rooms in the Aurora Palace which advertised itself as the swankiest hotel in town. For the first time in weeks, Jake and his partner wallowed in hot baths. Alluring smells assailed their senses as they luxuriated in foaming extravagance. A sumptuous meal followed.

Serena assured her two associates that once they discovered the revered headdress and delivered it safely to the appropriate authorities, she would make every effort to repay their kindness.

Jake was more interested in the form such reimbursement would take. Pecuniary settlement now came well down on his list. Enhancing his relationship with the lovely Mexican female by placing it on a more intimate footing had assumed a higher priority.

Buffalo Bob chuckled uproariously at his partner's ineptness when it came to cosying up to the high-born *viuda*. Jake had had little experience with ladies of such noble bearing. His only contact with the female sex had been gained in rough cathouses where money was the principal attraction for the calico queens.

Serena de Toledo handled her paramour's fumbled attempts at courtship with modesty and civility. But she made certain to keep their relationship on a friendly yet business footing. Jake's naïvety ensured that he was not disheartened.

So five days after leaving the bustling township, they found themselves approaching the seemingly impenetrable barrier of the Magdelena Mountains. Jake called a halt on the lip of a flat-topped mesa some 500 feet above the valley bottom. Somewhere within that gaunt fastness of interconnecting canyons was to be found the mysterious Valley of Trembling Rocks.

He removed the vital map from his coat and studied the scrawled delineation.

'You know this place?' enquired Serena optimistically, peering over his shoulder. Her musky scent wafted over the freighter, making it hard for him to concentrate.

'First time that either of us has passed this way,' he muttered, somewhat reluctant to stifle her eagerness. 'Let's hope that this map is accurate enough for us to find the right valley.' He pointed to a prominent landmark labelled the Devil's Finger. 'This pinnacle has to be the key. Find that and we'll be in the right place.'

'We must push on then,' the woman urged her associates. She nudged her mount forward towards the narrow cleft where the rough trail meandered down a steep gradient in a series of sharp zigzags.

Jake caught her up before she reached the start of the dangerous descent.

'No need for us to hurry,' he suggested. 'That headdress has been hidden for over three hundred years already. A few extra days ain't going to make any difference.'

'That is where you are wrong, *Señor* Fontelle,' replied the woman with vigour.

Jake quickly cut her short. 'Now that we are getting better acquainted, how's about you calling me Jake?'

'As you will,' said the woman, somewhat impatiently waving her hand before continuing. 'But my devious husband has the original map. I made this rough copy while he was engaged in his diabolical ceremony. I gave it to

Don Alvarez.' Serena's fervent gaze held Jake with its hypnotic charisma. 'When Manuel discovered my brother-in-law had escaped and that I also had fled, he must have sent trusted men after him to retrieve the map. Now that his plan has failed, he will waste no time in coming after us. Even now he could be hot on our trail. That is why we must hurry.'

'Gee, ma'am!' Jake's left eyebrow lifted in surprise. 'Guess that lazy streak I'm saddled with has gagged my brains, seeing as I hadn't given it much thought. I didn't think your husband would launch a search this far north into American territory.' He released a heavy sigh. A sudden shiver rippled down his spine on recognizing the gravity of the perilous undertaking with which he had landed himself and his partner. 'I should have known he wouldn't let the theft of his precious map go unchallenged.'

'Believe me, Jake.' Doña Serena smiled. Her radiant features lit up momentarily before assuming a more serious aspect as she emphasized her worries in a compelling manner. 'The crossing of the border into America will not deter the Shadows of Montezuma from preventing anybody else gaining possession of that precious icon. It is central to their odious plan to stir up revolution among the peasant farmers.'

Jake nodded his head vigorously. 'Then what are we waiting for?' Without further ado he led the group in single file down the perilous trail.

The arduous nature of the terrain through which they would have to pass was no place for a wagon. It was fortunate that Buffalo Bob was acquainted with the livery stable proprietor in Williamsburg who had been willing to do a deal: the wagon and team in exchange for three saddle ponies and a pack mule.

Safely on the broken sagebrush plain below the mesa, all eyes focused upon the surging mass of the Magdelenas. Somewhere along that brutal upthrust of fractured sandstone lay the entrance to the hidden valley.

As the day progressed, they moved steadily further and further into the enclosing grip of the mountains. Towering blocks of bare rock hemmed them in on either side. Sagebrush gave way to mesquite and the creosote bush, with the occasional Joshua tree poking through the mass of boulders that had to be negotiated. Isolated columns thrust out of the sandy floor like the bones of ruined temples.

Jake studied the depiction on the map. Nothing bore the slightest resemblance to that which they were seeking. So they trudged wearily onwards moving ever deeper into the wild remote fastness.

Their pace inevitably slowed. Around noon of the third day Buffalo Bob let out a raucous howl of glee. His jabbing arm pointed to a soaring pinnacle of rock some half-mile ahead on the right side of the canyon they were following.

'Has to be the Devil's Finger,' he yelled, bouncing up and down on his saddle.

'You are right, *Señor* Buffalo,' enthused

Doña Serena, catching the old skinner's gusto. 'The map was right after all.'

'So this is the Canyon of Trembling Rocks,' murmured Jake, exhibiting a more cautious reaction. 'Now all we have to do is find the entrance to Green Valley. And that ain't gonna be no walk in the park, seeing as that darned headdress has been lying undiscovered for centuries.'

That piece of stark realism was received with muted nods from the other two explorers.

'Guess you're right, Lazy,' agreed Bob Cantrell. 'Old Montezuma sure wouldn't have advertised his hideout to the whole world. He will have chosen a place that only the most resolute searchers can have a chance of discovering.'

After reaching the base of the evocatively-named monolith, coffee was soon on the boil. Along with some cookies specially selected by a sweet-toothed Buffalo Bob, the brief snack provided the extra surge of energy needed for the search that followed. The upper region of the box canyon offered a myriad of concealed places from where access to the hidden valley might be gained.

None was obvious. And the map gave no hints as to how the entrance was to be identified. Only that it lay on the far side of the sandstone battlement.

'Where do we start?' enquired a baffled Bob Cantrell, scratching his thinning grey locks. 'It could take us another week to search this lot.' A listless arm swept the barren panorama.

'We must find it soon or Don Manuel and his followers will catch us up.' Serena rubbed her hands, concern etched deeply in her pinched features.

'Then we'd better split up and get started,' urged Jake. He divided up sections of the broken terrain for each of them to search.

For the rest of the afternoon they avidly scoured the lower reaches of the field of loose scree beneath the towering ramparts. When dark shadows of impending dusk made any further exploration dangerous, a halt was reluctantly agreed.

That night they camped beneath the looming presence of the striking marker. With the sun disappearing over the western profile of the rugged highlands, Jake poked at the fire, wondering what the following day would have in store.

His gaze flickered to the mesmeric vision on the far side of the cavorting flames. Never had a woman looked more beautiful. Black wavy hair framed the limpid features of a goddess whom no ancient tribe of Aztecs could ever have imagined. If the great Montezuma had chosen a princess to rule by his side she would have surely been related to this woman.

The mournful hoot of an owl broke into his ruminations. A potent warning that such thoughts were best left under wraps until their current task had been fulfilled.

Jake was the first to wake up next morning.

Dawn was breaking over the eastern rim. The Devil's Finger, baleful and unsettling, presented a black silhouette against the striations of colour scarring the early morning sky. As the sun rose above the parapet, the shadow of the monolith began to move. Slowly at first, it gradually extended across the canyon floor.

Jake was mesmerized by the strange sight. His eyes followed the shadows, which moved ever faster as the sun rose higher. Then the notion struck him like a thunderbolt. This was a sign from Montezuma himself. The elongated shadow of the pinnacle would point out the hidden entrance to Green Valley.

Quickly he shook the others awake.

'Look!' he shouted. 'The Finger, it's pointing the way.'

Enthused by the fervid excitement in his voice, they eagerly followed his own jabbing digit.

Bulging eyes followed the dramatic race of the shadow across the canyon. It was awesome to behold. Having reached the far side of the canyon, the shadow paused in its headlong flight. The upper-most tip lingered at one particular place.

Then, as quickly as it had formed, the lifelike image started to fade. In less than a minute the shadow had completely disappeared. With the sun slowly disappearing behind another bank of rocks, the spectacular exhibition was terminated for another day.

'Did you note its position?' Jake clamoured, eyes glued to the all-important spot.

'A narrow entrance must lie behind that bunch of trees along the base of the cliff over yonder,' enthused Bob. 'We've done found it, Lazy. Yahooooo!' The old guy began dancing a spirited jig. Jake couldn't help but join in.

Serena watched the two lively buddies cavorting around and singing out of tune. She shook her head laughing at their antics. 'Crazy gringos!'

An hour later, following an animated breakfast, they led their horses and the pack mule up the tortuous slope. Circling around tumbled boulders and squeezing through narrow cracks in the rocky downfall, they eventually reached the line of stunted trees at the base of the main cliff.

'You stay here while I take a look see,' Jake said, handing the paint's bridle to Buffalo. Then he pushed through the dense undergrowth.

Fifteen minutes later he emerged some fifty yards further along the narrow ledge. Animated gestures indicated to the others that he had found the concealed entrance.

'It looks to me like a tunnel has been dug through the mountain,' he informed his associates. 'No way is that a natural cave. The walls are too smooth and there are marks that must have been made by hand tools.'

'How far does it reach?' asked Bob.

'I only went in a short distance,' Jake replied, 'but it must be a fair length to penetrate right through to the far side. So we'll need some torches to light our way.'

'Good job I added brands to the supply list,' said Bob, delving into the burro's pack. 'The store clerk told me these were guaranteed to last a full hour before they need resoaking in lamp oil.'

Pushing their way through the bushes, it was clear that nobody had passed this way recently. Probably since Montezuma himself had discovered the mysterious tunnel. Axes were required to hack away the thick undergrowth to enable the animals to pass through. The entrance to the tunnel was only just high enough to accommodate horses and riders moving in single file.

Bob shivered as he stared at the sinister black hole. 'If'n there's one thing I hate it's being closed in,' he burbled. 'It gives me the creeps. I've spent my whole life in the open. How some fellas can willingly go underground every day to work in mines beats me.'

'Just think of all that lovely loot that's lying around out there waiting for some enterprising jiggers to find.' Before he'd even finished the remark, Jake cursed his overactive mouth. He coughed out a nervous laugh in a desperate attempt to cover his incaution. 'Maybe there'll be something left for us to salvage once we've found Montezuma's headdress.' For the benefit of Serena he added firmly, 'After all, that's the main reason for this expedition.'

Bob caught on to his buddy's angle. 'Sure is,' he agreed. 'We wouldn't want the goods for ourselves.'

It was lucky that Serena only heard part of the exchange. She was examining the marks on the walls.

'You're right about these being made by people,' she remarked, running an elegant finger along the grooves. 'I'd say they are even older than the period of Montezuma. They were probably hacked out by the original inhabitants of these barren lands.'

'Is that possible?' replied her sceptical admirer. 'This must have been a mighty big undertaking for primitive Indians to achieve.'

The woman snorted with indignation. 'My ancestors were extremely competent at building and organizing their communities. Legends have passed down through the centuries proving that they were related to the kings of ancient Egypt. Carving out a tunnel like this would have presented no difficulties to such far-sighted people.'

That certainly put Lazy Jake in his place. With a couple of unthinking comments, he had jumped from the frying pan into the fire. Quickly backtracking, he once again struggled to appease this beautiful yet feisty dame.

For the second time, Buffalo Bob came to his aid.

'We ain't got time to discuss ancient history,' he warbled trying to conceal a hearty chortle. 'Let's ride, else those Shadowy varmints will be snapping at our heels.'

The old skinner struck a vesta and ignited his torch. He sucked in a deep lungful of air and muttered a silent prayer under his breath before leading the way into the Stygian blackness of the tunnel.

'Well, here goes. Let's hope I don't have a panic attack afore we reach daylight.'

The constricted passage stretched for about a half-mile in an arrow-straight line. So narrow was the cutting that their saddle-bags rubbed against the sides, and their heads were forced down to avoid painful contact with the roof.

Bob emitted a huge sigh of relief when he spotted the tiny pinprick of light that heralded the end of his torment. The trio emerged into welcome sunshine and a valley that defied all the laws of nature. Spread out before them was a veritable utopia. Green was the dominant colour, with trees and lush vegetation everywhere. A creek flowing down the middle of the hidden oasis provided all the water necessary for maintaining such a verdant paradise.

'So now we know why it's called the Green Valley,' muttered Jake, who was as bewildered as his associates.

'And we must be the first people to set eyes on this heavenly place since the great Montezuma himself discovered it,' Serena whispered, her dulcet tones displaying an awestruck reverence. She slowly dismounted as if in a trance and walked to the edge of the rock shelf overlooking the hidden gem.

'Not for long, lady,' rasped old Buffalo, jolting the woman from her entranced reverie, 'if'n we don't shift our asses and find that headdress purty damn quick.' Bob tipped his battered hat. 'Pardon my French, ma'am.'

'Y-you are right, *Señor* Buffalo,' stammered the Mexican *señora*. 'We cannot afford to waste time with the Shadows close behind.'

A narrow trail meandered down into the lower pastures. Rabbits scampered around. Deer also were in profusion as well as wrens, quail and wild turkeys. But evidence of human settlement was absent. They rode along beside the creek to the far end before turning around to retrace their steps. Barely a word was uttered, so intent were they on absorbing the mesmeric spectacle that Mother Nature had created.

Having reached their destination,

Jake surmised that it shouldn't be long before they found the all-important cave in which the revered icon had supposedly been secreted.

7

Lost . . .

On the far side of Green Valley, Charlie Moon was becoming ever more prickly. His partner was falling further behind. Growling and muttering under his breath like the crazy mutt he was, the surly outlaw at last decided to give voice to his grievances. He slowed his mount to a walk, allowing Turner to draw level.

'Go much slower and that posse is bound to catch up,' the Dog complained. 'Why can't you keep up? That flea-bitten nag is almost going backwards.'

'Ain't my fault he took a bullet.' Tincup slung a thumb to the sorrel's flank, now dripping with blood. 'Fact is, the poor critter is done for. We're gonna have to ride double.' Without waiting for any objections, Turner dismounted and drew his pistol. 'Sorry about this, fella,' he sighed, patting the woebegone cayuse on its lathered neck. 'Better that we end it now than you keeling over in an hour's time. And Charlie's right. We need to make better time to evade that posse.'

'Cut the jawing, Tincup,' rasped Moon, 'and get it over with.'

The little guy issued a further sigh of reluctance, then cocked the Navy Colt and jammed the muzzle against the sorrel's head. 'Goodbye, old friend,' came the despondent mutter. Then he pulled the trigger.

Without uttering a sound, the horse crumpled to the ground. Turner retrieved his rifle and saddle-bags. He was reluctant to abandon the saddle which he'd had for the last four years. It was now almost part of him. But there was no way it could be toted riding double.

'Hurry it up,' scowled Moon irritably.

The Dog was less than enthralled at having to place the extra weight on his own mount. Unless they could secure his partner another horse by the end of the day, both of them would be cast afoot. Such a prospect did not bear thinking about in this desolate country.

But that is exactly what happened.

Under normal circumstances the sturdy bay could handle any terrain. But four days with very little water and grain had weakened the animal. Even the insignificant extra weight of a stringbean like Tincup Turner was having a detrimental effect on its stamina. And so far, no isolated farmstead or trading post had been encountered.

Although he refused to acknowledge it, the truth was that Charlie Moon was lost. He knew that he should not have taken that side trail. His idea had been to hoodwink the posse. But the devious plan had gone awry. The trail had petered out after the first day. Now they could be anyplace. All they could do was to keep heading north; and by his calculation they ought to cut the

Albuquerque-Gallop road eventually.

The trouble was that his own horse was now on its last legs.

An hour later, what he had dreaded suddenly became reality. The bay's front legs faltered. The animal stumbled a couple more times before issuing a mournful whinny and going down. Both men were thrown off. Desperately, as if hoping to delay the inevitable, the poor creature struggled to get back on to its shaky legs.

But it was to no avail. Sensing that the end was nigh, a pitiful neigh issued from the animal's mouth.

Minutes later following another termination, the two outlaws were forced to continue their desperate journey on foot.

'We'll have to cross the mountains to reach the main trail,' Moon informed his partner, setting off up a gentle gradient. Tincup grudgingly followed in his wake.

Much to their discomfort, it rapidly became apparent that riding boots were not designed for prolonged walking.

Moon tried to make light of their predicament. 'Don't worry,' he assured his sidekick. 'I reckon we can't be far from the Albuquerque road. It's just over that ridge.' He pointed to the scalloped ramparts ahead. 'Ten miles at the most should see us hitching a ride on the stagecoach.' A wily smirk warped his lined face as he struggled to maintain an optimistic spirit. 'We might even be able to rob it.'

Tincup did not share his partner's optimism.

Onward and upward they tramped.

Overhead, the swirling clouds had fused into an eerie greyness. Loose skeins drifted down from the leaden sky, enveloping the bones of the wild landscape giving it a sinister feel.

Adding further to their woes, it began to rain. Within minutes a full-blown storm had settled over the Magdalenas. Without the necessary clothing, they were soon soaked to the skin. Progress slowed measurably.

Dank clouds had by now obscured the ridge line, making life even tougher. What would otherwise have been a relatively simple if uncomfortable trek was becoming a perilous ordeal. Emerging from the shelter of a ravine on to a level plateau, the wind clutched at their thin clothing.

'You know where we are, Charlie?' Tincup's plaintive enquiry was met with the accustomed scornful retort from the Crazy Dog.

'Of course I do,' he snapped. 'I once passed through these mountains heading for Arizona.' But that had been five years before when the weather was favourable.

They continued to stumble along. Hour followed hour with no let-up in the storm. Cold was becoming a serious issue for them both. If they did not find dry shelter soon . . . Moon thrust the lethal notion to the back of his mind. It didn't bear thinking on.

'Can't be much further,' he threw back to his buddy. But the words were snatched away by the buffeting wind. He wished now that he'd kept to small jobs instead of aiming to join the big league.

He flapped his arms, trying to generate some much-needed warmth. The movement made him realize that he no longer had the shotgun. A curse gurgled in his throat. It must have slipped from his benumbed fingers. And he hadn't even noticed.

A trail of muddy footprints in their wake were fast disappearing as the downpour intensified. The only positive aspect of this calamity was that, being summer, it was not snowing. But that was no consolation when you were lost amidst this wild and forbidding terrain.

Tincup suddenly slipped on a wet rock and went down. A cry of anguish brought his truculent partner to a halt.

'Get up!' Moon growled out above the howling of the wind. 'We ain't got time to rest up.'

'It's my ankle.' Turner winced, his grubby features creasing up with the pain. 'I think it's broken.'

'That's all we need,' complained Moon. 'Lean on me. We can't stay here.'

The little weasel staggered to his feet and slung an arm around his partner's shoulder. From then on, progress ground to a shuffling crawl.

Another hour passed. The light was beginning to fade. Everything around them was grey and without form. More serious, however, with the approach of night they were feeling much colder because of their saturated condition. Without adequate dry clothing, a night in the open didn't bear thinking about.

'I can't go any further,' Tincup gasped out, sinking to the wet ground. Head bowed, he blurted out the inevitable. 'We're going to die, ain't we?'

'Don't talk eyewash,' Moon responded with a vigour he didn't feel. 'Can't be much further now.' He flapped his arms like a demented windmill trying to generate some warmth.

'Leave me here,' Turner groaned. 'I'm only slowing you down. Maybe

100

when you get out of this mess, you can bring help.'

Much as the Crazy Dog would have loved to do just that, he did not want to be left alone in this inhospitable wilderness. He was about to hoist his buddy up when he heard it. At first he thought his dulled brain was playing tricks. Straining ears pricked up. Then it came again.

The low yet unmistakable rumble of human voices. They were coming from just below the crest of the hill where they now found themselves.

8

. . . And Found

The cave offered a dry place to shelter from the storm that had suddenly blown up. Buffalo was dragging on his old corncob pipe, trying to keep it alight. Wheezing sucks produced a thin spiral of blue smoke that dribbled from the corner of his mouth.

'That thing will be the death of you.'

Jake's comment received an apt rejoinder that characterized their loose friendship.

'You should talk,' Cantrell responded. 'The stink from those cheroots would stun a gopher at ten miles.'

Crouched side by side in the entrance to the cave, they continued exchanging acid remarks. Serena shook her head in bewilderment. She would never understand the Americano sense of humour.

It was early evening and the light was dwindling as dusk approached. They had been forced to seek shelter in the nearest cave when the storm broke.

Huge slivers of lightning crackled across the darkening sky. They were followed by the deep rumble of thunder.

Bob shivered. 'I hope those rocks don't decide this is a good time to flex their muscles,' he muttered, pulling harder on the pipe.

Jake shared his concerns but kept them to himself.

He was not in the best of moods. For two days the trio had searched every nook and cranny in the vicinity. Yet still they had found no evidence that the Aztecs had been anywhere near the Green Valley. His disappointment was written indelibly across the contours of his face.

'You don't think the map could be a fake, do you?' Bob posited to his partner.

Serena butted in, angry at the

suggestion. She was not so down-hearted as her companions. 'I can assure you that the map is genuine. The icon has to be around here somewhere.' Her stoical features brooked no dissent. 'We just need to find it.'

Jake lit up another cheroot and took a sip of hot coffee. The woman's optimism was infectious. 'Maybe we've been looking at this all wrong,' he ventured.

Before he had chance to consider their situation further, a faint noise impinged upon his senses. It was coming from outside the cave where they were holed up.

'Listen!' he hissed, gesturing for silence.

'What?' asked Bob.

'Voices! Can't you hear them?' stressed Jake.

Bob shook his head. Both men cocked their heads to one side, listening intently. Nothing. Only the keening of the fretful wind disturbed the quiet.

'There,' Jake called out again. 'You

must have heard it that time.'

Bob nodded. 'You're right. It seems to be coming from above. Do you think those Shadow dudes have caught up?'

Jake shook his head. 'It's the wrong direction. I reckon that somebody must have gotten lost in the storm. Get your slicker. They sound like they need help.'

Leaving Serena, they scrambled out into the rain, making their way up a slippery slope on to the plateau above. Dank mist obscured everything.

'Hello!' Jake called out. 'Can you hear me?'

There was a choking reply as two hazy shapes emerged from the gloom. The two men were in desperate straits.

'Thank the Lord you found us,' gasped an exhausted Tincup Turner. 'We got ourselves lost attempting a short cut across the mountains trying to reach the Albuquerque road. If'n you hadn't come along, we'd have been goners for sure.'

Even the Crazy Dog was grateful to have found other human beings. But he stayed quiet, keeping a firm grip on the butt of his pistol.

Bob led them back down to the safety of the cave where the two outlaws immediately huddled around the warmth of the fire. Serena poured them each a welcome mug of coffee. In the flickering light, both parties studied one another. Jake was puzzling over the reason that had made these two desperate characters attempt such a hazardous undertaking.

Following another coffee and some much-needed food, Moon was the first to recover. He walked over to the cave entrance and peered out.

Shades of night slid across the hazy landscape. A crafty glint in his eyes was hidden from his rescuers as the devious felon figured out how best to work this piece of good fortune to his advantage. These dudes no doubt had horses and supplies. There was no chance of leaving today. He quickly made a surreptitious gesture for Turner to keep quiet about their real situation.

Serena examined the older guy's

ankle pronouncing it no more than a sprain as she bandaged it up firmly.

'Much obliged, ma'am,' the old-timer gushed. 'That sure is a relief. I figured it was broken.'

Jake gave voice to his suspicions regarding the sudden appearance of the strange duo. He clutched a cheroot between his teeth. 'So why didn't you stick to the main trail? These mountains are unforgiving to those that don't know them.'

'We are prospectors heading for a new strike north of Albuquerque,' said Moon confidently. The lies slipped easily off his oily tongue. 'We would have gotten there too if'n the nags hadn't given out on us. Then we got lost in this durned storm.'

Moon settled back, eyeing the other men over the rim of his mug.

The big dude looked capable enough. He was the one to watch, unlike his buddy, a washed-out old jasper who could easily be rubbed out. And the woman, a right stunner even if she was a greaser. Maybe, once they'd gotten rid of these hicks, a little fun could be enjoyed.

The leery smirk sent a cold shiver down Serena's spine. She hunched closer to Jake. The woman's near proximity made him tingle.

Both men had hidden plans for this Mexican *belleza*, but with completely different intentions in mind.

The stilted conversation dwindled as Jake eyed the two outlaws. Something here was not quite right. He could sense a tension between them. They would both need watching. It was Moon who broke the uneasy silence.

'So what are you guys doing in this bleak spot?' he enquired casually. The question was aimed at Buffalo.

'Just a spot of digging,' replied Bob without thought. 'We're hoping to find — '

' — some good hunting!' Jake quickly interjected arrowing a look of keen caution at his partner. 'These hills are reckoned to be ripe with game. We've been here a couple of days.'

But Moon was no dimwit. There was no evidence of any prey in the cave. He quickly caught on to the fact that the two 'hunters' were not what they seemed. And even if they proved so to be, why would a woman wish to tag along? He kept the knowledge to himself. All would be revealed in good time.

* * *

'Keep the noise down!' grunted Don Manuel de Toledo as he struggled up the steep rocky slope below where he expected to find the final resting place of the sacrosanct Aztec icon. 'We're almost there. Another quarter mile and we should find what we're after. We know that the gringo thieves have got here ahead of us seeing as their horses are down below. No warning must be given to alert them to our presence. That way we can take them by surprise.'

The other eight members of the

Shadows of Montezuma followed him. The loose nature of the terrain, however, made it virtually impossible to remain silent.

With the original map in his possession, the Mexican grandee had made better progress than expected. Discreet questioning in El Paso and Williamsburg had confirmed his expectations that they were hot on the heels of their quarry.

When the surviving ambushers had reported their failure to retrieve the hastily copied map from his brother, Manuel had rightly concluded that his rescuers would seek to appropriate the icon for themselves. He had lost no time in responding.

A couple of like-minded associates and their peons had immediately been organized to set off in pursuit. The long-lost headdress of Montezuma could not be allowed to fall into the hands of those who would seek to thwart his revolutionary ambitions.

He was particularly incensed, and

not a little worried, to discover that his wife had absconded from the hacienda. In view of her violent objection to his plans, he was sure that Serena was involved in some way.

Meanwhile, up in the cave, Charlie Moon had risen early.

A fitful dozing was the best he had managed during the night. The outlaw stretched out the stiffness in his limbs, then moved over to the cave entrance. He peered outside. At least the rain had stopped. Even a weak sun was trying to make its presence felt. As soon as it was fully light, he and Tincup would be off.

Moon lovingly fondled the Remington on his hip. He drew the gun and pointed the weapon into the dim interior. With no witnesses to report their presence, they could make good their escape to start up again elsewhere.

The Mad Dog's ugly chortle was cut short by a scraping outside the cave. It sounded like a clatter of falling stones. He pricked up his ears. A muted curse floated up from the scree slope below.

Who could be out there at this hour? Had one of the others risen before him? He hurried back into the cave and counted four motionless bodies.

Then it struck him. A posse must have followed their trail across the mountains and somehow found its way into the valley below. Definitely not a welcome sight. He hauled out the revolver and checked the loading. The indeterminate rattle of stones resolved itself into a line of nine figures shuffling up the grade. In less than five minutes they would reach the cave. Something had to be done. And quickly.

Then he remembered the woman. A bargaining tool.

Gun in hand, Moon hustled back into the cave and dragged Serena out from beneath her blanket.

'On your feet, gal!' he snapped, waving the pistol in her face.

Serena screamed. The strident yell brought the others to wakefulness.

'What in tarnation is going on?' demanded Jake when he saw the ugly snout of the revolver jammed hard against Serena's head. The terrified look on her face prevented any retaliation.

'I knew there was some'n funny about you, mister,' growled Buffalo, stumbling to his feet.

'Keep away if'n you don't want me to use this thing.' The skunk's shaky voice was laced with panic. Flinging an arm around Serena's neck he pulled her towards the cave entrance. 'Now stay back!' he rasped.

'Careful, Charlie,' coaxed Tincup, knowing that his partner was easily capable of living up to his nickname if confronted. An angry sidewinder, he would spit venom without a moment's hesitation. 'You don't want to do anything stupid, do you?'

Moon scowled. 'That warning includes you as well, Turner. Don't think I wouldn't drop you if'n I had to.'

At the cave entrance Moon prodded the woman out into the open for those approaching to see that he meant business. Then he shouted for the advancing posse to stop. 'That's far enough,' he called out. 'I have a gun here and I'm not afraid to use it.' Hiding behind the woman he went on, 'There's no way that you lawdogs will take me alive without the woman getting hurt. So keep your distance.'

The Shadows drew to a halt, frozen in time like statues. Then they all dived for cover behind a tumble of boulders.

'*Madre de Dios!*' exclaimed Esteban Cortez, who was Manuel's second-in-command. 'Who in thunder is that?'

'Looks like the *bufon* thinks we are a posse,' another expressed with a laugh.

'Then he must be a bandit on the run,' added Esteban, joining in the hilarity.

'Silence!' growled their leader. 'Can't you see that they have captured Doña Serena?'

The shock was evident in his trembling voice as he recognized his wife. This was no joking matter. The leader of the Shadows was stunned to discover that Serena was being held hostage. Being a proud Mexican grandee, Manuel could not afford to lose face by allowing such an insult to go unchallenged. His men would expect no less of their leader.

'So what are we going to do, Master?' asked Esteban respectfully.

Manuel thought for a moment before expressing his decision. Somehow, this bandit had come across Serena and had taken her hostage for just such an eventuality as this.

'Spread out around the entrance and keep under cover,' he hissed. 'We don't know how many are in there, or whether they have found the headdress. And make no mistake, *compadres*, we are not leaving here without it. Or my *esposa*.'

But for the time being they were stuck. It was a stand-off.

Although his wife was being held as a bargaining tool, it was the Aztec icon that had to take precedence. The guys up there thought they were the law, so why not continue that deception?

He turned back to address those in the cave.

'This is Sheriff Mather from El Paso,'

he called out, assuming an American accent. 'The game is up, mister. You can't escape. Let the woman go and I'll see that you are fairly treated.'

The response was immediate. A .44 slug kicked up gravel inches from Manuel's face. He hugged the ground along with the others.

'Come any closer and the next one is for the woman.' Laced with menace, the quivering threat also oozed panic. 'I've killed once so I ain't got nothing to lose.'

Manuel recognized that here was a desperate outlaw who was capable of anything. A wild animal cornered.

'OK, mister,' he replied, struggling to maintain an even yet incisive tone. 'No need for any more shooting. But we are not going anywhere. And neither are you. They don't call me Mulehead Mather for nothing. And I always get my man.'

The response to the Mexican's defiant claim was another bullet whining off a nearby rock.

'That's your answer, tinstar,' Moon guffawed.

He pushed the girl back inside the cave, settling himself near the entrance. Gun in hand he had them all covered. 'Now throw your guns down,' he demanded. 'And no funny tricks. Bring them over here, Turner, and remember that you're in this up to your neck.' The thought made the crazed galoot chortle. 'If'n that sheriff takes us in, make no mistake, it'll be a rope's end for the both of us.'

'What the heck is this all about?' rapped an angry Jake Fontelle, fuming at his impotence to do anything.

'Never you mind that, sucker,' came back the caustic rejoinder. 'Just remember that it's me holding all the aces.'

Jake placed a comforting arm around Serena's shoulders. Beneath the coat he had given her, the slim body trembled uncontrollably.

Moon sneered. 'You sweet on the dame, mister? Can't say that I blame you. She sure is a peach.' The outlaw's acerbic jibe saw Jake scrambling to his feet. He made to lunge at the grinning skunk. Only the quick reaction of Buffalo Bob saved him from terminal injury.

'Take it easy, Jake,' the grizzled skinner muttered quietly, holding his partner back. 'Remember your moniker — Lazy by name, lazy by nature, which means reining in your temper. This varmint ain't worth the hassle.'

'That's right, old-timer,' snarled Moon, jabbing his gun at them. 'I ain't worth a bean. Not one miserly cent. All this trouble for nothing.' His piggy eyes glazed over. 'All I ever wanted was one big job and my reputation would be assured. But that stupid bank clerk in Carrizozo had to play the hero and spoil it all.'

Jake pressed him to continue. Anything to keep the bastard occupied.

Then it all came out. The whole sordid business.

'Now you can see that I ain't got nothing to lose.' The bitter outpouring having finally run its course, it didn't make the Crazy Dog feel any better. It just made him realize that there was no going back. Whatever the outcome, he was determined that a long spell in jail was not an option to be considered. 'However you look at it,' the outlaw grumbled, the pistol dangling from limp fingers, 'I'm dead meat. So don't try anything stupid. A few extra dead bodies don't bother me none.'

The crooked smile was all the more chilling for its lack of humour, a grim reminder that here was one desperado hopelessly beyond recall.

Once again they settled down to play the waiting game.

It was Serena who broke the silence. 'The man outside who called himself Sheriff Mather ... ' She paused, lowering her voice further so that the outlaws could not hear. 'I knew I'd heard that voice before. And it isn't Dave Mather who is out there.'

Jake sat up quickly. 'Go on,' he urged the woman.

'That is my husband, Manuel de Toledo. He has caught us up much sooner than I expected. That Americano accent is feigned. He often adopts it to impress his business associates.'

'Better we keep this to ourselves,' advised Jake in a hoarse whisper. 'Any talk of a precious icon and this guy might decide to throw in his lot with the Shadows. And then our goose would be well and truly cooked to a frazzle.'

'So what do we do?' Serena was almost in tears. The panic in her voice carried across to the far side of the cave. But she didn't care. 'We're trapped. A group of revolutionary fanatics out there and a gun-crazy bandit in here.'

She glared at Moon, almost willing him to pull the trigger. But it was all show. She didn't want to die. This honourable and resilient man beside her was worth ten Don Manuels. And she did not want to lose him now. Lucky for them, talk of religious fanatics had not registered with Charlie Moon.

'Better keep the dame under control, fella,' stressed the outlaw, brandishing his revolver. 'That is if'n you want to wake up tomorrow.'

Tomorrow! The thought made Serena cringe. Another day in this tomb, it didn't bear contemplating. In more congenial surroundings she could have enjoyed the company of Jake Fontelle. Waves of self-pity were cut short by an all too familiar voice from outside.

'You in the cave! Time is running out.' The brusque words of Don Manuel echoed round the cave. 'We will give you until noon to surrender. After that expect no mercy.'

'How much time have we?' asked Buffalo Bob.

Jake peered at his pocket watch. 'Less than two hours.' Then in a conspiratorial whisper he added, 'Whatever happens, this dude has to keep thinking that the law is out there otherwise the game's up.' Serena gave him a questioning look. 'Those guys won't want to leave any witnesses when they find the icon. And you've convinced me that it has to be around here somewhere.'

That was when a gleam came into the eyes of Tincup Turner. The ex-prospector had become more and more withdrawn as time had passed. Now suddenly he became animated. 'There could be a way out of here,' he suggested.

The others were all ears.

'What do you mean?' The controlled enquiry could not hide the hint of excitement in Jake's voice.

9

Breakthrough

Turner had moved to the rear of the cave and was examining the apparently solid wall. He rubbed his hand across the rough surface.

'Before figuring out there were easier ways to make a living, I was a prospector up in Colorado,' the little dude explained. 'I earned a reputation for being able to recognize the best rock formations likely to deliver paydirt. They weren't always rich seams. But I did make one fortune in gold up in the town where I got my nickname. The trouble was, I lost it all. The usual thing — the three Ds.'

Puzzled looks brought a grin to Turner's crinkled contours.

'Dames, drink and dice, not necessarily in that order.' His eyes glazed over as distant memories were resurrected. 'I was with a buddy of mine called Jim Taylor who scooped a tin cup of water from the creek. And lo and behold, there were flakes of gold in the bottom. That's how it all began.'

'Get to the nitty gritty,' rapped an impatient Charlie Moon. 'What has this blamed history lesson to do with us coming out of here in one piece?'

Tincup ignored the retort. He lit up a quirly before continuing.

'I'm certain this cave is not a natural formation.' He picked up a smouldering branch off the fire to illuminate the section of wall he had been studying. A finger jabbed at a distinctive grey streak. Turner's gap-toothed smile found the others staring at the striation. 'Lead ore known as galena,' said Turner, eager to display his knowledge. 'Thin, which probably means that the miners had reached the limit of the seam so they shut it down.'

'How does that help us?' persisted a sceptical Charlie Moon.

'If'n the cave narrows to a rubble-choked flue at the end, then we're in business,'

Turner replied. He scrambled along the narrow passage to its apparent termination. There he pointed out what he had hoped to find. 'Eureka!' he exclaimed. 'Didn't I tell you?'

'He's right,' Bob concurred, examining the plethora of boulders that blocked off any further progress. 'All we can pray for now is that the tunnel continues on the far side.'

'And this lot ain't too thick,' added Jake removing his coat. Bob joined him, along with Tincup. But Moon remained where he was.

'You ain't scared of a little hard graft, are you, fella?' sneered Bob. Tincup added his own leery smirk to the biting jibe.

'I've done my fair share of labouring,' the outlaw snapped back angrily. Although he omitted to mention that all the lifting had been of other people's property. 'You guys ain't gonna catch me out that easy.' He hefted the Remington. 'I'll sit here and supervise, make sure nobody gets any ideas. So you guys better get a shift on. Time is running out.'

The Crazy Dog certainly wasn't wrong there. The others, including Serena, began scrabbling at the piled-up boulders.

To begin with, it was a difficult task to move any of the rocks. After such a length of time, possibly centuries, they were jammed tighter than a bank vault. Sweat rolled down their straining faces. Fingernails broke and tempers frayed while all strived fruitlessly to lever the stubborn critters apart.

Eventually, however, after much cussing and grunting the tide began to turn. One by one the rocks were levered out. But the task seemed endless. It was Tincup who finally made the breakthrough when he stumbled forward, his hand clawing at a small hole no bigger than a fist.

'We're through,' he shouted. Exhilaration registered in his excited voice. His claim had been justified.

The hole was quickly enlarged sufficiently for a man to climb through.

Jake took it upon himself to investigate what lay beyond the barrier. He searched the small chamber carefully, eager peepers probing every nook and cranny. The flickering light of his torch cast deep shadows, lending an eerie feel to the exploration. His head spun with the heavy atmosphere.

Then he saw it.

A leather bag with strange markings on it. His face assumed a puzzled look. What could it be? He jammed the torch into a crack, slowly unfastened the gold clasp and opened the bag.

What he discovered inside elicited a startled gasp of surprise.

'Some'n wrong, old buddy?' A concerned Buffalo Bob stuck his head into the aperture. 'What have you found?'

For a moment Jake was lost for words as he gazed on the priceless artefact. Scepticism regarding the Aztec head-dress of Montezuma had festered in his mind while they had failed to find it. Had the thing ever really existed?

Now here he was holding it in his hands. Precious gems twinkled in the light cast by the torch. Rubies, blood-red, winked at him. Emeralds green as grass played havoc with his vision. And gold inlay, hidden for centuries, once more displayed its hypnotic allure. So this was what the Shadows of Montezuma were after. And no wonder.

Another call from his partner brought Jake Fontelle back to the year 1877. He gingerly passed the icon through to Bob. Eyes popped as they all stared agape at the headdress. Even Charlie Moon was awestruck, rendered speechless in the presence of this masterpiece of Aztec artistry.

But only for a moment.

Here was his chance to redeem some self-respect. But most of all, to make a good profit after all the things that had gone wrong in recent weeks. While the others were held spellbound by the mesmeric appearance of the headdress, the cold glint of greed edged the Dog's profile.

Barely above a whisper he hissed, 'I'll take that.' The gun was pointed at Bob's head. The old guy snarled. His body tensed as he pondered whether he should refuse.

'Better hand it over,' a subdued Jake Fontelle advised, reading his partner's mind. 'No sense getting your head blown off.'

'Good advice, mister,' said Moon. Then to his own partner, he said, 'Come over here, Tincup, and help me out. This piece of loot is gonna repay us for all this hassle.'

The prospector felt the Crazy Dog's eyes skewering him to the cave floor. He hesitated. What should he do? Go with Moon and be on the run for the rest of his life? Or side with the others and face a murder rap? When it came down to a choice, there was only one course open to a dude like him. He moved across to stand beside Moon. Reluctantly, but the decision had been made.

'Now let's get out of here,' ordered the surly outlaw, indicating for Jake to lead the way along the newly discovered tunnel.

Buffalo Bob followed, ashen-faced.

This was his ultimate nightmare. Entombed in a narrow passage. What if'n he got stuck? The thought brought on a touch of the shakes. He closed his eyes. *Pull yourself together, damn it!* he muttered to himself. This was no time for cracking up. Nobody noticed anything untoward. This was one bogey that Bob had kept to himself.

'Don't get too far ahead,' Moon called out.

'Don't you trust me?' came back the pained reply from Jake.

'Too right I don't,' snarled the outlaw, pushing his partner ahead. 'Now get moving, and watch their asses.'

Edging their way forward, the small procession entered the main tunnel. The torch brands lit the way. Up ahead, Serena paused in awed silence, thinking of times past. 'Just think,' she said. 'Men once laboured here in frightful conditions. We are the first humans to pass through in centuries.'

Charlie Moon broke into her thoughts. His harsh growl echoed down the tunnel.

'Keep moving. We ain't got time to hang around jawing.'

Serena shuffled onwards. None of them knew where the tunnel would end, or if there had been a rock fall during the intervening years. That scenario didn't bear contemplating. Now that the reality of what they were facing had sunk in, even Moon began to wonder if'n he ought to have taken his chances in a shoot-out with the law.

After an hour, Jake called a halt, much to Moon's aggravation. They all slumped down on the wet ground.

'We need to rest,' he insisted. He uncorked a water bottle and handed it to Serena. 'Especially your buddy with that sprained ankle.'

Moon scowled. 'Five minutes and no more.'

All too soon he had them back on their feet. Time passed in a blurry haze. In this claustrophobic atmosphere of perpetual darkness, day and night meant nothing. And the flickering glow from the torches was starting to fade.

★ ★ ★

Outside in the open air, Manuel de Toledo glanced at his watch. He signalled for his men to move up towards the cave entrance. Taking advantage of every scrap of cover available, he inched closer to the dark threshold.

'You guys in there have had long enough,' he shouted out, injecting a stern measure of grim determination into the command. 'Throw out your weapons where we can see them. Then come out with your hands high.'

He waited. But there was no response.

'You hear me?' he repeated impatiently. 'Surrender now or face the consequences.'

What was going on in there? Maybe they wanted him to charge, then pick off his men when they were in the open. Well, two could play at that game.

'Chavez!' he hissed, gesticulating for a lanky follower to join him. 'You are a hunter?' The man nodded. 'I want you to take a couple of men and gather up half a dozen rattlesnakes and put them in a bag. That should flush those critters out.'

'*Sí, patrón*,' replied Chavez. 'Ees good plan.' Then he hurried away.

Twenty minutes later he was back with a wriggling sack.

'Get as close to the entrance as possible, then fling the sack inside,' Manuel ordered him. 'That should bring them out. We will cover you.'

The group followed the tentative progress of their confederate as he crept ever nearer to the cave entrance. Still there was no sign of any movement. Skirting the edge of the dark opening, Chavez unfastened the neck of the sack and threw it inside. The hiss and rattling of the deadly serpents carried down to those watching. If that didn't provoke a response, then something serious was amiss.

Time passed but still nothing happened.

Manuel swallowed nervously. He cursed silently but realized that he had no choice: a frontal assault led by him was necessary to retain his authority. Gritting his teeth the Shadows' leader crept ever closer to the cave. But no way was he going in there before those durned snakes had been neutralized.

Chavez was once again given his orders, this time to clear the cave. A simple peon he might have been, but the Mexican was no fool. Going in there could earn him a bullet for his trouble.

Toledo openly scorned his hesitation. 'There cannot now be anybody in there, you fool,' he railed at the wavering man. 'If the rattlers didn't provoke a reaction, the gringos must have discovered a back way out. So don't be such a coward. Get in there and do what has to be done.'

A forked stick clutched in their hands, Chavez and an associate hustled up the slope. A series of thuds and hisses were followed by the dead serpents being tossed out into the open.

The Mexican then appeared, signalling for the others to join him.

The cave was indeed empty. And it only took them a few minutes to discover the reason. Manuel scrambled through the narrow aperture at the back and shone his torch around. As it shed light on the empty leather bag he snatched it up. A manic curse echoed through the confines of the tunnel. The thieves had stolen the revered Aztec icon and escaped through a hidden passage.

The leader of the Shadows had no compunction in labelling them thieves. The headdress was essential to gather the believers into proclaiming a new dawn of enlightenment for Mexico. The simple peasants would then believe its wearer to be the living embodiment of Montezuma.

But there was no use dreaming of a new age when the means of achieving that end was in the hands of his adversaries.

'Unscrupulous robbers have stolen the most sacred possession of our Lord and Master, the all-powerful Montezuma,' the Shadow leader ranted, waving the empty bag in the faces of his followers. 'We cannot allow them to escape with it, can we?' A murmur of spirited agreement greeted his passionate declaration.

'Then forward, my loyal and gallant followers.' He led the way over the loose scattering of rocks and through the narrow opening into the tunnel. 'There is no time to lose,' he urged them, lighting another of the torches. 'Those thieves have a head start. But if we hurry, there is a good chance that we can avert this catastrophe.'

They set off at a rapid pace, encouraged by the knowledge that others had recently passed this way.

★ ★ ★

After what seemed like an eternity the tunnel began to bend in a series of zigzags. At the same time it was widening out and pit props became more frequent. Total darkness was dissolving into a haze of grey. Jake could now pick out the shadowy outlines of his associates.

'We must be getting close to the exit,' observed Buffalo. Blessed relief edged his comment.

As they continued along the dripping passage, Jake whispered into Serena's ear. 'Move a bit faster. I have an idea how we can rid ourselves of these skunks.'

'What do you have in mind?' the woman replied, her interest piqued.

'I've noticed that around each of the bends, there is a recess. It must be where the miners stored their tools and took a rest so as not to block the passageway. I reckon that if'n I hide in one, I could jump Moon when he passes.'

A worried expression clouded the woman's face. 'He is a dangerous man, Jake. A thug like that would shoot you down without a second thought.'

Instinctively, she stroked his stubbled cheek. Her touch was overwhelming. As was the smile that followed. 'And just when we are becoming better acquainted.'

Jake returned the smile. He kissed her hand as their eyes met for that brief moment of intimacy. Then it was back to the business of thwarting Crazy Dog Charlie Moon.

'Don't you fret none, honey,' he reassured Serena, 'I have no intention of getting shot. But we have to do something.'

'Well, you be careful.' She squeezed his arm as he slid into the next alcove.

Old Bob, stumbling along behind, failed to spot the subterfuge as he moved by in the darkness. Minutes passed. But Moon and his puny confederate failed to appear. Jake listened intently but could hear nothing. He waited another minute, then warily peered around the edge of his hideout.

Before he knew what was happening a hand grabbed his hair and rammed his head against the corner post. A strangled gurgle erupted from his throat as he was flung to the ground. A match flared as a torch was lit.

The Dog's leering face filled his vision.

'Thought you could get the better of Charlie Moon, eh?' sneered the outlaw, quickly relieving Jake of his revolver. His feverish eyes blazed. The gun's muzzle prodded Jake's head. 'Well, you failed. And now it's pay-back time.' The revolver ratcheted to full cock.

Through the murk of his subconscious, Jake knew that his end had come. After all he'd been through and now to be shot down by this scumbag in some festering mine. They say that your whole life flits past at such times. All Jake Fontelle saw was a blinding flash followed by a deafening roar.

Then absolute darkness engulfed him.

10

Tincup the Turner

The blast of the gun discharged inside the mine had shocked them all.

Having been ahead of his buddy, Bob had automatically assumed that Jake was following close behind. The sudden ear-splitting roar of gunfire came as a shock. And it could only have come from the outlaws. There was no way that the Shadows could have made such fast progress.

Jake must have tried to outwit the cunning rat. Turning round, all Bob could see was blackness. He immediately hurried back to ascertain what had occurred.

On reaching the zigzags he slowed his pace. The skunk could be waiting to gun him down just round the next corner. Although now dimming rapidly, the torch would give him away. He paused at the next bend before continuing. What should he do? The old skinner was in a quandary.

He decided to call out and hope for some kind of reaction to his presence. 'You OK, Jake?' The query was muted and tremulous.

A grating shuffle informed him that all was not well, otherwise his friend would have replied. 'Don't come any closer, Moon,' he croaked out, 'else I'll bash your brain out with this club.'

In truth he was completely unarmed. But the outlaws weren't to know that.

The reaction to his toothless threat had an unexpected meekness.

'Charlie tried to kill your partner,' came the frail voice of the little runt known as Tincup Turner. 'I stopped him just in time.'

'Is Jake alive?' asked a worried Buffalo Bob.

'Yeah, he's still breathing,' Turner confirmed. 'Moon got off a shot that struck him in the head, but I can't tell how bad it is. We have to get him out.'

Bob was undecided. 'How do I know you ain't just waiting to blast me when I show myself?'

Turner's response was to throw two guns into a position where Bob could see them. 'Now I'm unarmed,' replied the prospector. 'You best come here and help me get this jasper outside.'

The skinner stuck one of the revolvers in his empty holster and palmed the other. Gingerly he peered round the corner to ensure this critter was not trying to trick him. Everything appeared just as Turner had said.

Bob wasted no further time. He hustled back along the passage to see Tincup leaning over the comatose Jake. Blood was running down his ashen face. To one side was the unconscious body of Crazy Dog Moon.

'Guess you were telling the truth after all,' Bob conceded. 'Although I ain't gotten a notion as to what made you switch sides.'

'I'll explain later,' said Turner, 'when

we've gotten this fella outside.'

A rumbling deep within the mountain did not bode well.

'Sounds like the storm has caused a landslide. This valley is known for them,' Bob stammered, helping his new associate to lift the inert form of Jake Fontelle. 'We better get out of here quick before it brings the whole lot down about our ears.' Claustrophobic terror was written across his haunted features.

'So the legend about the Valley of Trembling Rocks is true,' remarked Turner.

Bob didn't reply. His entire being was focused upon reaching the open air.

Once they had safely left the suffocating confines of the old mine, Buffalo Bob laid his injured partner on the ground. Serena fussed around, anxious to determine the extent of this brave *hombre*'s injuries. She dribbled water over the dirt-smeared face wiping away the congealing blood.

A groan elicited a sigh of relief that

the injured man was coming round. Once his face had been cleaned up it was clear that Jake had been lucky. The bullet had only creased his skull. He would be left with a groove across his head but no permanent damage appeared to have been caused.

Jake tried to sit up, but Serena pushed him back down.

'You need rest after being attacked like that,' she purred.

'Don't worry,' Buffalo assured her with a cheeky grin. He planted a lighted stogie in his partner's mouth. 'This guy has a hide thicker than a rhinoceros and with the brains to match.'

Jake offered a smile. But the effort brought a pained wince to his pale features.

'Take it easy, pard,' Bob soothed. His gaze shifted to the little weasel hovering in the background.

The old skinner swung his pistol to cover the outlaw. Turner nervously fingered the small tin cup hanging on a leather thong round his scrawny neck.

It was a good luck charm given to him following his first big strike in the town that gave him his nickname. Tincup had worn it ever since. He figured that removing it would seal his fate. Three pairs of eyes held him in their frosty grip.

It was Buffalo Bob who voiced the doubts they were all chewing over.

'So why have you suddenly decided to double-cross your sidekick?' he challenged, keeping the guy covered while Serena bandaged up Jake's head. Betraying a trust was anathema to the proud Kentuckian, even where a skunk like Charlie Moon was involved. 'And it better be good.'

'I'd already decided to quit running with Charlie after he botched our last job in Carrizozo.' Tincup shook his head as he recalled the failed robbery. He explained the circumstances briefly before continuing: 'He was figuring to move into the big league by robbing banks. He even talked about doing train jobs. But we ended up fleeing for our lives with nothing to show for it.'

'So is there a posse on your tail?' Jake croaked out. He'd been listening in to the turncoat's confession.

'I sure wouldn't be surprised,' replied the outlaw. 'After Charlie gunned down that bank teller, the whole town was out for revenge. Charlie wanted the reputation of a notorious bandit. All I wanted was to grab enough dough to live the easy life. Prospecting is too much like hard work. Then he went and got us lost in that storm. Coming across you when we did saved us from a miserable end.'

'It was lucky that we heard you on the ridge above the cave,' interrupted Jake.

Turner nodded his agreement. 'And I sure was grateful to meeting up with you guys. But not Charlie Moon!' Tincup spat out a terse growl. 'All that Crazy Dog wanted was to kill you all and snatch the headdress. Far as I was concerned, that was one step too far. I wanted out. But I had to wait for the right opportunity of turning the tables on him. So when I saw him getting set to ambush your partner in the tunnel I knew what had to be done.'

Bob listened to the story, carefully assessing the guy's sincerity. He certainly appeared genuine in his remorse.

'Do you think I can trust you with this?' he said, handing his gun back to the reformed outlaw.

'I've done with bucking the law,' Turner stressed. He accepted the weapon and dropped it into his holster. 'If'n I get out of this in one piece my plan is to head back to Colorado. Hear tell there's been a big silver strike up in Ouray. Prospecting might be harder, but it has its compensations. Maybe I'll strike it rich again.'

'And maybe we'll join you.' Bob nodded. 'What do you say, Lazy?'

'We still have to get out of here before those Shadow dudes catch up,' Jake reminded his partner. 'And they ain't going to be long in coming through that tunnel once they find out we've scarpered with the headdress.'

'Guess you're right there,' Bob agreed. He cast a searching eye across the terrain where the tunnel exit had emerged. 'Looks like we've come out further along Green Valley. I could double back and get the horses while you rest up here. We ain't gonna get far without them.'

Jake agreed. He peered at his pocket watch which surprisingly had not been broken during the attempt on his life. It read 11.45 a.m.

'The Shadows will have discovered that the cave is empty. They are also bound to find the empty bag.' Jake's comment held a distinct note of apprehension.

'Manuel will not be pleased,' muttered Serena in pessimistic accord, 'that his precious icon is now in our hands.'

Bob wasted no more time listening to his associates discussing the issue. He set off back along the edge of the cliff face at a fast pace.

A clear track took a gently shelving

line down through the tree cover towards where the horses were teth- ered. This had clearly been a well-used route at one time by the previous inhabitants of the valley. It was now a deer run. Bob was in such a hurry that he didn't bother to tread carefully. Slipping and sliding, he somehow managed to maintain his footing on the shale-covered slope.

Within ten minutes he was back close to where they had arrived the day before. And there were the horses. He could just make them out through the trees and shrubbery. Eager to get back to the plateau above, he stepped out confidently.

The ominous rumble coming from inside Ladron Mountain did not appear to have affected the valley. All was quiet down here.

★　★　★

Jose Vasquez was bored. Why did the Master always put him in charge of looking after the horses? On numerous occasions during their pursuit of the stolen map he had been left holding the reins while the others enjoyed themselves in El Paso and Williamsburg. Sure, they had brought him food and drink, even a fat *señorita* on one occasion. But he would have much preferred to paint the town red with his *amigos*.

He leant against the trunk of a tree, his head lolling in the warmth of the morning sun. The storm had passed although Ledron Mountain was still growling out his displeasure. For once, Jose was glad to have been left behind.

Then he heard it.

No more than a few stones rattling. It could be a deer. Although such creatures would quickly identify the presence of a human by his smell and keep well away. The Shadow slid further down into the cover of some bushes. Carefully he palmed a lethal Bowie knife from the sheath around his waist. Sharp eyes probed the deer trail.

There it was again, and coming nearer. Then he heard a grunt.

It was of human origin.

Knuckles blanched white, Jose gripped the bone handle tightly.

On the far side of the clearing he spotted a man pushing his way through the bushes into the open. It was a gringo, and he was old enough to be Jose's father. This man was clearly one of the thieves who were out to steal the Aztec icon. Somehow they must have escaped detection. And now this one had come back to retrieve their cayuses.

The Mexican smiled as he circled around on the outer edge of the clearing to get behind the intruder. He allowed the gringo to pass before moving into the open. Unfortunately he stepped on a dry twig.

The sharp snap alerted Buffalo Bob. The older man swung round just in time to see a flash of steel aiming for his back. Instinct took over, and he spun away from the deadly blade as it skimmed past his shoulder. It ripped

151

the cloth of his shirt. He felt a painful nick as the keen edge tickled the skin of his neck.

Jose growled. His moustache twitched in frustration at having missed his target.

The sudden attack had caught Bob off balance. He fell to the ground rolling on to his back. Scrambling crablike away from his attacker, the skinner palmed his own knife.

Jose saw the move and paused. Now he knew that it would be a fight to the death.

Bob clambered to his feet. Both men eyed each other like hungry predators. Hunched down, arms bent at the elbows, they circled around the killing ground. No words were spoken. Concentration was etched on each man's face as he carefully weighed up his foe.

Jose made a feinting lunge. But Bob saw it coming and stepped back. Five minutes passed as each man tried to trick the other into exposing himself. Jose was taken aback that the older man was so agile.

But being a young man, the Mexican was impatient to finish the gladiatorial contest. He growled and spat, unlike Bob who maintained a calm demeanour, waiting for the opening he knew would surely come.

Knife fighting was second nature to the old skinner. He knew all the tricks. Skinning buffalo had made him adept at knife work, not least defending his haul against thieving hunters who wanted to avoid the hard graft.

His chance came when Jose attempted a scything lunge at his opponent's head. He expected Bob to bend away to his right, thus allowing the Mexican to deliver a left hook to the chin setting him up for the final *coup de grâce*.

Bob saw the manoeuvre coming and quickly ducked down in the opposite direction. The glinting blade whistled by overhead, throwing Jose off balance. His torso was left completely exposed. Bob took this golden opportunity and struck upwards.

The blade sank deep. A look of total

surprise registered on the simple Mexican's face as he peered down at the blood dribbling from the fatal wound. He staggered back clutching the hilt. Death was moments away. The Mexican wheezed and groaned as his life slipped away.

Bob stooped down over the dying man figuring he had enough time to enquire about the other Shadows.

'You cannot escape, gringo,' the man croaked, knowing his end was near. He coughed. A plume of bright red poured from his mouth. 'Montezuma will avenge himself on those who steal his sacred headdress. The Master is already inside Ladron. He will catch and kill you all . . . '

A final sigh heralded the peon's end as a final choking breath hissed from between gritted teeth.

Bob retrieved his knife and casually wiped the blade on his victim's shirt. The fight had wasted too much time already. But it had taken more out of him than he expected. Suddenly his legs felt like putty. He sank to the ground drawing in gulps of air. It was five minutes before he felt able to stand. A few puffs on his trusty corncob helped settle his nerves.

'You're getting a mite too long in the tooth for this, Bob,' the skinner muttered to himself while gathering up the reins of all the horses. He then mounted his own sorrel and led the rest of the remuda up the track in single file.

Hauling the bunch of horses up the slippery grade was exhausting. It took Bob longer than his earlier descent. So it was over an hour before he crested the rim of the valley.

'What kept you?' asked a puzzled Jake Fontelle. 'We were thinking you'd had an accident.'

Bob slid off his horse and sank to the ground. 'Any of that coffee left?' he mumbled. 'I'm plumb tuckered out.'

Serena noted the old timer's waxy pallor.

'He doesn't look too good,' she observed to the other two men.

'That's cos I had a bit of trouble down there,' Bob informed them.

'What happened?'

'No time for explanations now,' Bob replied, getting to his feet. He slung down the mug of coffee and mounted up.

Jake took another glance at his watch and realized that the deadline given by the leader of the Shadows had long since passed.

'Those critters can't be far behind now. We'd best be hitting the trail. These nags of their'n can be released once we're out of this valley.'

'Sounds like the mountain is about to blow as well,' Bob added as they departed, heading off in a northerly direction. The grumbling and cracking was growing in strength. 'Let's hope it traps those varmints inside.'

It was to be a futile expectation.

11

Ladron Speaks

The Shadows were making steady progress through the mine tunnel when a low rumble reverberated through the rocky fastness. It brought the single file stumbling to an abrupt halt.

'What ees that?' a fearful voice piped up as dust trickled down on to their heads. The lyrical flutter of the nervous exclamation would have sounded funny on a music hall stage. But here in the gloomy depths of the earth, it bore a spine-tingling resonance.

Nobody answered as another growl of protest boomed out. This one was much louder and shook the ground upon which they were standing. It felt like Ladron Mountain itself was issuing a challenge to those seeking to trespass within its hallowed depths.

A feeling of alarm gripped the superstitious Mexicans.

'Montezuma is angry at those who have invaded his sanctuary,' burbled one simple peasant follower. 'We should never have come here.'

'Ladron is girding his loins to teach us all a lesson,' howled a tormented Goliath of a man called Gigante. The others murmured their assent, recognizing that if the giant was afraid they all had reason to worry. Milling about like wayward sheep, the men shuffled their feet uncomfortably.

But Manuel de Toledo knew different.

More important, he needed to regain control of these simpletons immediately before they panicked. The rumbling was caused by the trembling rocks in the outer canyon, which had been displaced by the thunderstorm. A lightning bolt must have struck the unstable rock and set a landslide in motion.

Knowledgeable sources in Williamsburg had informed him that the phenomenon was usually minor and of a limited duration. But that was of little consolation when you were experiencing it at first hand. He knew they had to get out of this suffocating prison *rápidamente* before the roof of the mine came crashing down and buried them.

He figured that they must have come more than halfway through the mine. So it was better to carry on, but at a much faster pace.

'This is only an earth tremor,' he rapped out, effectively silencing the mumbling whinges. 'It has nothing whatsoever to do with the legend of Montezuma. And if anyone else causes unwarranted fear by going to pieces, I will shoot him down like a mad cur. Savvy?'

The Master's blistering gaze held the shuffling peons in a potent grip of steel. Fearful nods assured Manuel of their obedience. They were more afraid of him than any landslide. Even Gigante acquiesced to his fierce retort.

'*Bueno!*' Toledo spat out with vigour. 'Then let's get moving. And no more talk of rousing Montezuma's anger. Our spiritual guide would never do such a thing to his loyal followers.' Manuel smiled to himself. This last comment had been a sudden flash of inspiration.

He nodded for Esteban to lead off while he brought up the rear to ensure nobody held back. Yet much as he tried to affect an air of the domineering *jefe supremo*, Manuel was scared. He had heard stories about the trembling rocks and the devastation they could cause, none of which he had believed at the time. Until now.

Being trapped in this subterranean hell in the middle of such a thunderous commotion was a nightmare he did not want any of his underlings to witness. Terror warped the noble features into a hideous caricature. Hence the decision to bring up the rear. The Shadows trudged onwards, each man silently praying for deliverance from this hell-inspired mausoleum.

It was some time later that his

second-in-command tripped over an obstruction in the tunnel. Cortez cried out, bringing the shambling column to another halt.

'What is the matter now?' snarled the irate Shadow chief, pushing his way to the front of the line.

'Look, Master,' said Esteban, pointing to the prostrate figure lying on the ground.

The burning torch illuminated a man lying on the floor. Toledo toed the figure with his boot. A groan issued from the stirring form; it tried to sit up. He was a stocky varmint with a scar across his nose.

'Get the skunk on his feet,' Manuel ordered, 'and let us see what we have here.' At that moment the mountain issued another compelling roar of disapproval. 'Juan and Chavez,' he snapped at the two nearest men, not bothering to conceal the edgy rasp in his voice. 'Keep a close watch on the gringo until we escape from this ghastly tomb. We can question him once we're outside.'

Dust billowed along the constricted passage, urging them to increase their pace. It was clear that the tunnel was in imminent danger of collapsing.

At long last they stumbled outside, sucking in great lungfuls of clean air. Moments later a muted roar echoed down the tunnel. Their exit from the mine had been none too soon. Black dust poured out of the narrow crack as the rock buckled and twisted. The entire front of the mine then split from the rock face. Riving and grinding with fury, it tore asunder, effectively sealing off the whole mine.

Unfortunately, the two Shadows bringing up the rear were caught in the deadly upheaval. Their screams of terror were drowned out by the thunderous roar of falling rock. The survivors, including a stunned Charlie Moon, gave thanks to their guardian angels for the good fortune that had been bestowed upon them. Although for how long that would continue, Moon was now wondering.

He did not have long to find out.

Now that his ordeal was over, Manuel assumed his normal imperious manner. He stood over the sullen outlaw, glaring at him.

'You were one of the thieves who stole our sacred icon.'

The blunt remark was a statement rather than a question. Moon ignored the implication, instead making his own morose comment.

'You must be the posse from Carrizozo. Me and my buddy thought we'd given you the slip by taking a short cut over the mountains.'

Esteban Cortez couldn't resist a chuckle. 'This gringo still harbours the notion that we are the law.'

The others joined in the hilarity. But Manuel was not amused.

So this was the *bastardo* who had nearly killed him, and also held his wife hostage. He grabbed the smirking outlaw by his hair and dragged him to his feet. A hard slap rattled Moon's teeth.

'I do not take kindly to being shot at,' Toledo snarled. A gun suddenly appeared

163

in his hand and was jammed into the outlaw's neck. 'Give me one good reason why I should not kill you right now.'

The Crazy Dog gurgled. His life was in the balance. If he wanted to continue breathing he had to think quickly. It was all the fault of that double-dealing Tincup Turner. Moon promised himself to book the treacherous Judas an appointment with the Grim Reaper. It could only have been that skunk who slugged him. Nobody else was behind at the time.

'I can lead you to the varmints who stole your precious headdress.' He spoke up without any hesitation. 'There are four of them, including the woman, and I heard the leader say where they intended making for once they had escaped from the mine.'

'And where was that?' enquired Toledo, his interest stimulated.

The outlaw raised a bushy eyebrow. 'I ain't no mug, buddy,' he huffed, wiping the blood from his split lip. 'If I disclose that, you'll have no more use for me. I'll

spill the beans when the time is right.'
Moon was playing with fire and he
knew it. So he added, 'And it won't cost
you a durned thing.'

'Why would you help us if not to save
your worthless skin?' rapped Toledo.

'It was my partner who clubbed me
back in there.' The Crazy Dog thumbed
an irate digit to the devastation behind
as he growled out, 'I have a score to
settle with that skunk, that involves a
bellyful of lead.'

Toledo gritted his teeth. He was not
convinced. Nor was he concerned with
irrelevant vows of revenge. Being held
to ransom by a lowlife bandit did not sit
well with the lordly grandee. The
revolver rose, a snarl of rage presaging
the end for Charlie Moon.

But a reprieve arrived from an
unlikely source. Cortez closed down the
Shadow leader's reckless action. 'This
hombre is right, Master,' he stressed.
'We need the information he has to
regain possession of the icon. And also
remember that we are two men down.

Another gun hand will come in useful.'

Toledo simmered down. His associate was right. This man would come in useful. An Americano could be a valuable asset to their cause. He could smooth the way through this unfamiliar country. He nodded, suddenly displaying an affable disposition.

'My apologies for doubting you, señor,' he said, helping the outlaw to his feet. 'But I needed to be certain that you would not betray us to the authorities.'

Moon laughed. 'That's the last thing I want. The law and Charlie Moon ain't exactly bosom buddies.'

'It is settled then? You can become an honorary member of the Shadows of Montezuma. And be assured that when we have regained possession of our sacred icon, you will be well rewarded.'

Moon's face cracked in a genial grin. That was what he wanted to hear. He would also remember that this snooty greaser had humiliated him in front of his men. That was a slight the outlaw would not forget in a hurry.

Manuel was eager to get after the thieves. He dispatched one of his men to bring the horses and their wrangler from down below the plateau in the Green Valley where they were tethered.

The man took longer than expected. Manuel was bristling with irritation. As time passed the thieves were getting further away.

When the man called Latigo Vegas returned, he was still on foot.

Toledo grabbed him. 'Where are the horses?' he snarled.

'Th-they have been st-stolen, Master,' stuttered the frightened underling. 'And Jose has been killed.' The other men gasped. 'He had been knifed in the belly. It is a bad omen.'

The jumpy murmuring among the Shadows was silenced by a withering look from their leader. He was more concerned about being left without the means to pursue their quarry. He cursed volubly. 'What are we to do now without horses?' he railed, feeling impotent.

Charlie Moon offered a solution.

'I know this country,' he said with confidence.

The bandit had only become lost because of the severity of the storm the previous day. Now that it had passed over, he could recognize distant landmarks. He pointed to a prominent peak to the north-east.

'That is El Cuervo.' He gave the Spanish name for raven; the towering pinnacle possessed a similar shape to the bird and dominated the landscape. 'I once called at a ranch near by where they break horses for the military.'

'But that is a different direction from the one taken by the thieves,' countered Toledo indicating the hoof-prints, which headed due north. 'We will lose much valuable time going that way.'

Moon was becoming frustrated with this stupid blockhead. He struggled to contain his irritation. All it needed was one word from the puffed-up greaser and he would be crowbait. Gently, and with unaccustomed restraint, he pressed his case.

'You want horses?' He didn't wait for the obvious reply. 'Then that is the nearest place. And also I know of a short cut beyond El Cuervo that will bring us out ahead of them.' He paused to allow this tasty snippet to sink in before adding, 'So I suggest we get walking right away if'n we're to reach the ranch by nightfall.'

12

Thy Cup Runneth Over

The group of riders trotted across the sandy plain. The rising dust cloud from eight sets of hoofs had forced them to wear bandannas across their faces. To an unsuspecting observer they gave all the signs of being a band of outlaws. But the leader was Sheriff Bud Lassiter. And this was a posse organized by the town council of Carrizozo following the abortive raid on their bank.

Such had been the shocked fury of the town's citizens that Lassiter had found no problem raising the posse. He was less enthusiastic at having the bank's manager foisted upon him. The mayor had insisted that Henry Allison be allowed to join the posse. After all, it was argued when Lassiter had objected, wasn't it his brother who had been shot down by the gang leader?

The sheriff could not contradict such a forceful contention. So now he was reluctantly stuck with the overweight pen-pusher. Allison was definitely more at home in an office than riding a horse.

The sheriff threw a jaded look towards his deputy. Hank Merlin understood. The banker was holding them back. A quick glance to the rear showed that he was once again lagging behind. What he could see of the rotund visage was coated in dusty sweat. Hints had been dropped when they passed through Pine Bluff and Socorro without success. Yet still he persisted in staying with the posse.

Lassiter had to admit that Allison was a doughty guy.

Nevertheless, it was frustrating for the lawmen. They needed to maintain a faster pace. Lassiter knew that the posse was on the right trail. Questions posed to the lawmen of both communities had revealed the vital information that two men had passed through recently. Such descriptions as they were able to give had confirmed the sheriff's suspicions. But he also knew that once the two fleeing outlaws reached the Magdalenas they could easily disappear amidst the myriad of canyons cutting a swath through the mountains.

A family of prairie dogs watched the line of riders pass by. Barking and cavorting on their hind legs, the strange creatures presented an amusing sight that always brought a smile to the sheriff's face.

Allison never even noticed. Head down, he was wondering where all this would end. Should he have left the pursuit of the killers to the professionals? No use in dwelling on such things now. He was here and would see it through to the bitter end.

★ ★ ★

It was late afternoon when the footweary Shadows and their new recruit arrived at the Bosque Peralta horse ranch. Toledo was growing more and more impatient as the hours passed. His hostile mood threatened to boil over. Charlie Moon kept assuring him that the ranch was just over the next hill. When it didn't appear the Shadow leader was all for finishing off the outlaw with no further ado.

Only the steadying influence of Esteban Cortez prevented an untimely demise. Without the outlaw, they would be in a far worse situation.

'This gringo is the only one who can secure horses and lead us out of this maze of canyons,' the Mexican stalwart stressed. 'We have to trust him.'

Placing his reliance on the shifty Americano did not sit well with the pompous grandee. Toledo continued to snort and grumble at their enforced delay. But he was prudent enough to realize that his second-in-command was right.

Moon knew that he had the whip hand. However, his loathing of the Shadow leader grew more intense as the complaints and threats to his life increased. Once they had secured horses and retrieved the icon, Charlie Moon promised himself, this lowlife varmint would get his comeuppance in the form of a lead sandwich.

Until that occasion arose, he would need to stifle any hunger for retribution.

Zeke Welland ran the horse ranch. Moon recalled him from his last foray in these parts. It was as well that the old bronco buster did not recognize him. Moon had been clean-shaven when he stole a prized stallion. The thick drooping moustache now effectively concealed his features.

Welland could not conceal his amusement at these critters being cast afoot. Hearty chortles greeted the new arrivals.

He had no fear of any retaliation from the Shadows. The approach of the horseless men had been spotted an hour before their arrival at the ranch. He was thus able to gather his men to offer a show of strength. The horse trader had learned from previous occasions when broncs had been stolen. His men were spread out and well armed to thwart any precipitate action by the Mexican.

The rancher did not trust greasers but managed to conceal his distaste behind a bluff reception.

'Howdy there, *muchachos*,' he called out. 'You seem to have mislaid something.' More giggles from the other busters.

'We were set upon by thieves who stole our horses,' blustered Toledo. 'It is lucky that we came upon your ranch in time. Our water is finished and we are tired. Are you able to sell us fresh mounts?'

'Sure can,' breezed Welland, 'provided you have good old American dollars.'

Toledo hooked out a wad of notes from his coat.

Welland nodded eagerly. 'I'm always ready to do business, no matter who turns up here.' The sneering remark went over the Mexican's head.

But Charlie Moon was well aware of the hidden meaning intended. He smiled to himself. Zeke Welland had not changed. Still the caustic old rogue he remembered.

'And perhaps you would provide me and my men with the hospitality for which you Americans are well known,' added the Shadows' leader. That caught Welland off guard. He squared his shoulders, acknowledging the compliment, not realizing that Toledo was playing him at his own game. 'I am the owner of a large hacienda,' continued the Mexican, 'and my *vaqueros* have always been treated very well during visits to your ranches.'

The Bosque rancher drew himself up. No way was he going to be seen as a mean-fisted guy by these mutts.

'Hey, Panhandle,' he immediately called over to his cook. 'Get these boys some of those fine enchiladas you're famous for.' Then to another buster, he said, 'And Cimarron. You got any jugs of moonshine stashed away in the bunkhouse?'

'Just made a fresh batch this morning, boss,' came back the ready reply.

'Then let's have us a party. We can talk over some prices at the same time.'

★   ★   ★

The sun was well over the summit of La Cuervo next morning before both factions struggled back to wakefulness. It had sure been a night to remember. Zeke Welland had made certain that a patriotic duty to his fellow man had been furthered, even if they were only greasers.

And Toledo was satisfied that he had struck a good deal for the fresh horses. But now he was anxious to be away in pursuit of his quarry. The Shadow was not the only one to be glad of a swift departure from Bosque Peralta. A disquieting event of the previous night's session had unnerved Charlie Moon.

He was thankful that only he and the rancher were awake at the time. They were on the third jug, inhibitions had been discarded, as also had Moon's hat. With his features fully exposed, Welland was giving him more than just a casual glance. His soused gaze narrowed on to the man opposite.

Moon stiffened uncomfortably.

'Ain't I seen you somewhere before, mister?' the rancher slurred, trying to maintain his focus. 'Seems like that mug of yourn is familiar.' His features screwed up in concentration.

Moon vehemently shook his head. 'I've never been in this part of the territory before.' His denial was emphatic. Nevertheless, he gave thanks that the knife scar had been acquired since their last encounter; it further changed his appearance.

Welland scratched his head. 'It'll come to me. Old Zeke never forgets a face.'

Don't I know it, mused the outlaw. A silent prayer went out to his Maker that on this occasion the elephantine memory would fail the rancher.

He was lucky. At that moment a horse in one of the corrals started whinnying.

Welland stood up. The memory test was put on hold. 'Guess I'd better see to the horses. We've been having trouble from a hungry mountain lion.' With that comment he departed.

The incident was not mentioned the next morning, much to the Dog's relief. He was glad to leave Bosque Peralta behind.

Around noon the group of riders came upon the Salinas Mission. White-washed walls glinted in the sunlight. It appeared to be only a small settlement, peopled by a handful of missionaries and Indians. Monks ran the station but employed managers to oversee the work.

The Shadows drew to a halt on a hill overlooking the settlement. Woebegone groups of Pueblo Indians could be seen tending the fields with the attentive supervisors close by to ensure that none of them shirked their tasks.

The mission stations had been established by the Spanish conquistadores to spread Catholicism and convert the Indians to a more ordered lifestyle. The work was hard, the regime strict. But standards of living were higher than in the villages. Even so, many peasants chose to abscond, hankering after more easygoing ways in the villages.

If one was caught punishments could be harsh. One such miscreant was at that very moment being subjected to a flogging by one of the supervisors.

Toledo ground his teeth. This was one of the reasons he had formed the Shadows of Montezuma. Many Indians still resented the Spanish interference in their lives. Such simple folk would be easy to manipulate once the revolution started. They would rally to his cause with little persuasion.

In the meantime here was one small mission station where he could begin work for his cause. The hated missionaries and their lackeys would present little opposition in the face of a heavily armed force of invaders. Toledo chose to think of his men as freedom fighters.

Quickly he explained his plan.

'Here is our chance, my loyal followers,' he adjured in stentorian tones, 'to strike a blow against the imperialists who have stolen this land from our noble country. The *pueblos* down there will be grateful when we free them from the heavy yoke of slavery to which they are being subjected. This is only the beginning of a much wider rebellion that will soon follow.' His eyes blazed with a fiery passion. 'Are you all with me?'

A raucous cry of accord brought a smile of satisfaction to their leader's face. Only Charlie Moon resented having to participate. Not for any altruistic reasons. His sole aim was revenge and the seizure of the treasured Aztec icon.

'Then draw your weapons and let us grind these accursed invaders into the dust.'

Drawn up in a line, the Shadows dug in their spurs and charged down the shallow slope. As they neared the mission, a roar of defiance erupted from their mouths. Guns roared. The supervisors were taken completely by surprise. The first one to be shot down was the man holding the savage bullwhip.

One of the riders leapt from his mount and freed the victim.

Others who put up any resistance were soon dispatched. Within minutes the whole attack was over. Indians milled about in disunity, uncomprehending as to what was happening. When the monks emerged from their prayers in the church, Toledo was ready to greet them. One who chose to remonstrate was instantly cut down.

The Indians soon got the message and listened attentively.

'You men of God have no place in the true New Mexico that will soon dominate this region. Go back from whence you came and tell your overlords that the Shadows of Montezuma are going to form the new government. We are here to free the simple people from your burdensome yoke of tyranny. All of this land will soon be conquered in the name of Montezuma. The Indians will rise up and revere us as the true descendants of the Aztec nation.'

The remaining monks could do little but shuffle their feet and nervously finger the crosses around their necks.

Some Indians cheered the rousing declaration. But most shrank away from these violent assailants. The mission might be stringent but it offered a secure haven and a good life. They were well aware that the one who had been punished was a troublemaker, a jealous love rival who had stabbed his neighbour in a fit of rage.

But the Shadows leader was convinced he had won them all over.

'When you talk of this day, tell others that it was Manuel de Toledo who set you free. I am the one who is destined to wear the revered crown of Montezuma.' With that he fired his gun into the air and galloped off. The other

Shadows echoed his stirring cry and followed in his wake.

The stunned community of Salinas was left behind to lick its wounds and ponder over what exactly had taken place here.

★　★　★

Afternoon was waning when Bud Lassiter spotted the white tower of the Salinas Mission. The church glinted in the lowering sunlight. He and his men were tired. The mission would offer them wholesome food and a proper bed for the night. Hymn singing and a few prayers in the church were a small price to pay for such comforts. This would be their first opportunity to rest up for a spell since leaving Carrizozo five days before.

The fact that the peaceful ambience of the mission had been violated was brought home with a bang when Bud spotted a line of bodies laid out in front of the church.

Linen cloths covering the five corpses were stained with blood. It was clear that violence had been perpetrated here, and in the not too distant past. The monks who ran the mission were in a turmoil of distress. The robed brethren were struggling to understand what had befallen their peaceful existence.

Only the abbot in charge remained calm. A stoic acceptance of the catastrophe as being ordained by God could be read into his serene countenance.

Nevertheless, Father Antonio Xavier was only too pleased to welcome the law officer and his posse. An atrocity had been committed that required the attention of a worldly response. He quickly outlined the heinous event that had taken place earlier in the day.

'Have you any idea who these killers could be?' Bud enquired. 'Only we're trailing a couple of bank robbers who have headed this way.'

The abbot considered the question

before shaking his head. 'The leader was a man of my race, señor. A grandee from a noble family, judging by his conduct. He claimed to be acting as an emissary of a revolutionary sect calling themselves the Shadows of Montezuma.'

'I heard talk about that bunch last month when I was after Black Sam McGee down in El Paso,' his deputy interrupted. 'Those varmints practise some perty evil ways from what's been said. Sacrificing sheep and dancing around a fire at midnight. I didn't take much heed of it until now.'

Bud frowned, his thick eyebrows meeting in the middle of his forehead. He nodded at his deputy. 'Looks like this group is planning to spread its poison north of the border.

'Don't worry, Father,' Bud assured the anxious monk, 'I'll inform the authorities at the next town. They will alert the governor. Toledo and his crazy fanatics will soon be rounded up and dealt with.'

That promise appeased the good

father, who invited them all to participate in the full range of resources offered by the mission.

An early start was deemed necessary next morning in view of the urgent need to reach Albuquerque. The town was still three days' hard riding to the north.

They had been on the trail non-stop for much of the morning when they drew close to Acoma Gap. It was a split in the rocky wall along which they had been riding. Scrub vegetation dominated by sagebrush, interspersed with the ubiquitous yucca plant, cloaked the arid terrain. This was a junction where four trails crossed. On the far side they would join with the main trail to Albuquerque.

But they were not alone in the bleak wilderness.

It was Hank Merlin who saw the rising plume of dust floating in the still air as they entered the Gap. It was coming from the far side of the junction.

'We've got company, Bud,' he announced,

pointing a finger towards the drifting yellow tendrils. A meeting with the other riders could not be avoided.

'Palm your hardware, boys,' he ordered, 'and keep your eyes peeled. This could be those skunks who raided the mission. But don't do anything without my say-so.'

The posse slowed its pace to a gentle trot as it approached the midpoint of the crossing. A bleached, barely decipherable signboard indicated the directions to various settlements: Albuquerque north, Socorro south, Quemado west and Santa Rosa east.

The posse drew to a halt. On seeing that there were only four in the group, Lassiter relaxed. His hand moved away from the six-shooter to rest on the saddle horn as he waited for the other group to draw near.

In the lead, Jake Fontelle's attitude when he caught sight of the other riders was anything but lazy. Being in possession of the priceless Aztec headdress was making him nervous. These guys could be innocent travellers. Then again, they might be road agents after easy pickings. Like the other body of horsemen, he slowed his pace.

Then, for a brief instant, the sun was reflected off the lawman's badge. Straight away Jake knew this must be the posse hunting for the Carrizozo bank robbers. He had nothing to fear. But his new associate now hunched low in the saddle with 'guilty' written across his forehead. Tincup Turner's face suddenly turned shingle grey.

Dropping back Jake pulled his horse in beside the wanted man. 'Are these guys likely to recognize you?' he whispered, noting Turner's twitchy demeanour.

'Can't see how,' the anxious owlhoot gulped. 'Our faces were masked.' All the same, the outlaw pulled his hat down to shade out his features. He was not taking any chances.

The hesitant response brought little comfort to either man. If it came to a showdown, Jake mused, which side would he back? That was a question to which there was as yet no answer.

Turner's gaze fastened on to the bulky rider at the rear of the posse. 'The fat dude at the back is the bank manager. It was his brother that Moon gunned down.'

'Then you'd better hope those masks did their job.'

There was no amicability in the remark. This guy was a bank robber even if he had reformed and saved Jake's life. When it came to the crunch, much as Jake would deplore doing it, he would have no option but to shop the galoot.

They closed with the other group who were waiting at the junction. Both factions faced one another, each assessing the other's potential for trouble.

'You guys heading far?' It was Bud Lassiter who made the first overture. His nickname of Hardknott was reflected in the terse query.

'Santa Fe,' Jake informed him. 'We have business to conduct there.' He didn't deign to furnish the details of their venture.

'I'm Sheriff Bud Lassiter in charge of this posse,' the lawman continued. 'We're in pursuit of two owlhoots who tried to rob the bank. They failed. But the teller was shot down when he fought back. You seen anything of these guys?'

Jake shook his head. 'You're the first people we've come across since leaving the Rawhide trading post on the far side of the Magdalenas. Sorry we can't be of help.'

Lassiter accepted the statement with a regretful sigh. 'Then we'll just have to keep looking. One of them has a distinctive white scar on his nose. The other is a little weasel. If'n you see them, I'd appreciate your reporting it to the nearest law office.'

'Sure thing, Sheriff,' Jake gave the assurance while hiding his relief as Lassiter led the posse in single file past them. It was a tight squeeze.

They were almost past when Henry Allison stopped beside Tincup Turner. His eyes bulged wide with shock.

Turning round in the saddle he called out. 'This rat is one of the killers.' An accusing finger jabbed at the memento hanging round Tincup's neck. 'I recognize that necklace he's wearing.'

'It weren't me,' the wanted man blurted out. 'Crazy Dog Moon was the killer.' Sheer panic at being fingered had driven common sense to the winds.

Ignoring the denial, Allison drew his pistol. It was his younger brother who had been so brutally slain. Both robbers were guilty in his eyes. Without thought, he fired twice in quick succession. One shot lifted Tincup's hat into the air, but the second took him in the neck.

The outlaw tumbled from the saddle, dead before his body hit the ground. Jake and the others were too stunned to do anything.

Not so Bud Lassiter. Ever the consummate professional, his reaction to the sudden flare-up was immediate. He shouted to his deputy. In no time, Jake and his remaining two companions were surrounded by the posse. Henry

Allison was unable to take part. This was the first time the portly banker had shot a man. He stumbled over to the side of the trail and heaved up the contents of his stomach.

'Looks like those two robbers must have split up,' observed Hank Merlin, ignoring his colleague while relieving the prisoners of their weapons. 'These varmints must be his new gang.'

'That so, mister?' rapped the sheriff, addressing Jake.

'No it ain't!' Jake's repudiation was emphatic. 'Me and my partners came across this critter by accident. His horse had given out and he was on foot when we found him. We had no idea that he was on the run.'

That was when Serena decided to add her voice in support.

'That is the truth, Sheriff,' she asserted, removing her hat allowing the raven locks to cascade over her slim shoulders.

The men stared open-mouthed. The last thing they had expected to see riding with an alleged bunch of outlaws was a woman. And a decidedly fine-looking one to boot. Serena smiled to herself, knowing that she now had the upper hand.

'I am Serena de Toledo.' Her tone was measured yet contained a degree of noble authority that commanded attention. 'These men are my escort. We are heading for Santa Fe to deliver a revered Aztec icon into the hands of the Mexican delegation there. I am sure you will agree that it is not safe for any woman to travel alone in this wild country when bandits are likely to prey on innocent travellers.'

Nods all round from the enraptured male posse.

However, the woman's admission of being related to the leader of the killers at the Salinas Mission brought a swift accusation from the lawman.

'So you are in league with the Shadows of Montezuma,' he snapped brusquely. 'A Mexican grandee by the name of Manuel de Toledo has attacked and killed members of the Salinas Mission in the name of his evil sect. Clearly this murderer is related to you.' It was a clear avowal of indictment. 'How do you answer that?'

This revelation was another mind-blowing shock that had evidently rattled Serena. Her mind was racing. So Manuel had escaped from the mine and was hard on their heels. But she quickly gathered her wits in response to the allegation.

'Sí, señor,' she pleaded. 'You are right. He is my husband. But it is not as you think. I discovered his scheming deceit and have paid the price.'

She raised her flowing locks to let the lawman see the bruises on her face. A gasp of indignation greeted this revelation. If there was one thing that frontier Americans abhorred, it was violence towards women.

'So you see, I am trying to thwart his plans for revolution in my country.' A hand then indicated her companions. 'And these two gentlemen have been helping me.'

She then proceeded to outline briefly the crux of the matter. Stress was laid on the fact that she and her companions were totally innocent of any wrongdoing. They had tried unsuccessfully to save the life of her brother-in-law. A promise had been made that they would find the Aztec icon and present it to the appropriate authorities.

The woman's dramatic account appeared to have been sufficient to persuade the sheriff of her bona fides. This was confirmed when Jake produced the icon. Again the posse men gasped in awe as they beheld the beauteous magnificence of the sacred Aztec emblem.

But they were not the only ones gazing down upon the headdress.

13

The Penasco Plough

Manuel and the Shadows were making their way along a little-known Indian trail. They had made good progress since leaving the killing ground of the Salinas Mission. Moon had assured the Mexican grandee that this was the best way to avoid any other travellers who might later report their intended direction. It also had the bonus of enabling them to get ahead of their quarry. Then it would just be a simple matter of laying an ambush. The headdress would be theirs for the taking.

Suddenly they heard the sharp report of two pistol shots. The ominous crackle had originated from the far side of the line of hills they were following. Gunfire invariably meant trouble.

Manuel signalled a halt and silence.

'What do you reckon that is?' he enquired of Moon in a wary voice. The outlaw had sneakily succeeded in wheedling his way into the Shadow leader's confidence.

'Only one way to find out,' averred the outlaw, drawing his revolver.

Without waiting to be given the go-ahead by Toledo, he gestured for Cortez and the big man, Gigante, to accompany him up to the ridgeline.

Toledo raised no objections to this assumption of authority. Moon was a practised gunslinger. The grandee assumed that he was capable of sussing out how best to deal with any difficult situations in his own country. Although Toledo always presented an aura of arrogance, he knew his limitations. He had led the attack on the mission knowing there would be little opposition. This situation could, however, be a lot more dangerous.

Hunkering down on the crest of the ridge, Moon signalled his associates to keep quiet as they peered down into the hollow of Acoma Gap. Smoke from a six-gun drifted in the still air. It was held by a dude at the rear of the column. Moon's back stiffened as he recognized the rotund frame of the Carrizozo bank manager.

Another shock awaited his probing gaze when he saw the dead body of Tincup Turner lying in the dust. The irony of the situation brought a mean smirk to the owlhoot's warped features. This must be the posse who was hunting him down. Somehow the manager had recognized the little weasel and gunned him down.

At least it saved him a job. Although Moon would have preferred to have been the one evening the score with his old buddy.

The posse had made surprisingly good time. But they were much too close on his tail for comfort. Meeting up with that skunk Fontelle and his buddy had further complicated the issue. Even though the other person in that group resembled a man, Moon instinctively knew that it had to be Serena Toledo.

'What we do, *señor?*' whispered Cortez. He had now deferred to the authority to the gringo. The Mexican likewise had noted the badge of the lawman at the front of the posse. Moon was thinking hard. There were eight in the posse. The sheriff and his men had Fontelle and his two associates surrounded.

Another smile broke across Moon's leathery features. He chuckled. Straight away he understood the error that had been made by the sheriff.

'What is so funny?' asked the bemused Gigante.

'That posse figures they've caught a gang of robbers and that my old partner was their leader. And do you know what?' The giant's face still registered a blank stare. 'That notion ain't too far from the goldarned truth.'

Only when the woman revealed her presence and Fontelle displayed the

Aztec headdress did the real truth hit home. The smile was instantly wiped from Moon's face. Those slick-talking jaspers had persuaded the lawman that they were on the level.

But worse was to come. Gigante had also recognized the grandee's wife. He suddenly became animated.

'That is Doña Serena!' he exclaimed, his words vibrating with panic. 'Those thieves have kidnapped the Master's *esposa* and the revered headdress. We must rescue her.'

The man made to scramble to his feet. Any consequences of the rash act were overlooked in the naïve dimwit's eager desire to gain favour in Toledo's eyes.

Moon grabbed for his arm. 'Get down, you durned fool,' he hissed. 'Do you want to get us all killed?'

The hulking greaser was not listening. He growled, struggling to free himself. Knowing that all their lives were now hanging in the balance, Moon quickly slammed the barrel of his revolver over the big man's head. It was a solid thwack. Gigante slumped down unconscious. Luckily, the fracas was too far distant for the sheriff and his men to have heard.

Continuing to observe the events being played out below, the outlaw realized the implications as both parties headed along the trail in the direction of Albuquerque. Whether the sheriff had arrested the others for stealing the icon, or they had joined together, it was impossible to determine. What mattered was that the Shadows were now up against a much bigger force.

Moon cursed under his breath. This meant that it was going to be a far tougher proposition to regain possession of the priceless treasure.

'Get this lunkhead down the slope,' Moon rapped, addressing Cortez, 'and tell the bossman we have a real task on our hands if'n he wants to get that headdress back.'

Moon watched the group of riders moving away. All he could do was grind his teeth in frustration. He spat in the dust.

The chances of this bunch of turkeys regaining the icon now had disappeared upon the desert wind. Unless he could figure out another angle, they were sunk. And Toledo would then see Charlie Moon as a liability and surplus to requirements.

His chances of emerging from this situation with his hide intact as well as a profit demanded quick thinking. Guile and cunning, which had kept the Crazy Dog one step ahead of the law all his adult life, were now put into action.

By the time he had slid down the back slope Moon had worked out a solution to turn the tables on the posse and its new complement.

Toledo was waiting below. His dour countenance did not bode well for the latest recruit to his cause. Hands on hips, he squared off, ready to berate the outlaw. Moon forestalled him by announcing that he had worked out the perfect solution.

Jake Fontelle joined Sheriff Bud Lassiter at the head of the new contingent as they headed north. He was glad of the extra company, which offered protection against any further attack by the Shadows. Just behind the leaders, Buffalo Bob rode side by side with Serena.

At the rear one of the posse men was leading Tincup Turner's horse with the dead man securely strapped across the saddle. A substantial reward had been offered by the bank for the capture of the outlaws. So the men were buoyant and cheerful. As the principal town of central New Mexico, Albuquerque would provide rest and relaxation for a couple of days before they headed south-east, back to Carrizozo.

It was towards noon of the following day when they came in sight of the phenomenon known as the Penasco Plough.

At this point the southern shoulder of

the Los Pinos mountains drove deep into the plains in the shape of a giant ploughshare. On the left side lay the direct trail heading north for Albuquerque. The right arm was far less accessible. A myriad of canyons cut through the Cibola Plateau. For those who knew the way through this challenging labyrinth, a short cut saved four days if Sante Fe was their objective.

Neither Jake nor his partner were confident enough to tackle the tortuous route. So they opted for Bud Lassiter's offer to escort them as far as Albuquerque, which was only a day's ride away.

The party had taken the left fork in the trail when a rider appeared from the other direction. He was galloping hard. When still a quarter-mile off he began shaking his sombrero to attract their attention. The rider's whole demeanour registered panic. Lassiter signalled for them to haul rein.

They waited for the rider to arrive. It was Esteban Cortez. He had been chosen by Toledo to make the approach to the posse, being the most reliable of his followers. Gasping for breath, the Mexican brought his lathered mount to a juddering halt.

'Please, please, *señors*,' he gabbled breathlessly, 'you must come quick.' Cortez pointed a gloved hand at Lassiter's badge of office. 'You are a lawman?' he asked.

'What's the problem?' Lassiter replied.

'A gang of *bandidos* has attacked a freight wagon in the canyon back there. I was passing on the ridge above and saw it all. But I am only one man.' He lifted his shoulders. 'What could I do? When I left the gang were ransacking it.'

'Any idea of their numbers?' said Lassiter, adopting a sternly formal manner.

'I could see three only, but one of them was referred to as Crazy Dog,' the Mexican warbled in a thickly layered accent.

'That's the other guy we're after,' crowed a thin beanpole called Lefty Boggs.

The rest of the posse perked up on

hearing this revelation. Dollar bills floated before their eyes. Crazy Dog Charlie Moon's capture, dead or alive, was worth double that of Tincup Turner.

'We didn't hear no gunfire,' called a sceptical voice from the rear.

'That is because the outlaws caught them by surprise,' replied Cortez, who was ready for this objection.

'How far up the canyon is this?' rapped Lassiter.

'No more than a half-hour's ride,' the wily Mexican assured him. 'But you will need to hurry before they leave.'

'What we waiting for, boys?' Boggs called out, swinging his mount towards the right-hand trail.

'You guys OK to carry on north?' Lassiter enquired of his new associates. 'We'll catch you up soon as this business is sorted.'

'Sure thing, Sheriff,' Jake assured him. 'You get up there.'

'OK, mister, you lead the way,' Lassiter said to the newcomer.

'I cannot come with you, *señor*,' Cortez protested. 'I am in big hurry. Boss wants me back at ranchero pretty damned quick.' Without saying another word he spurred his mount away, heading south in the direction of Salinas.

'Be seeing you.' The Mexican waved a cheery hand. The triumphant grin that cracked his swarthy features was hidden from the lawman. In truth, the Mexican hoped never to set eyes on the posse again.

His aim was to continue south until the posse was out of sight. He would then circle back behind a line of crags to rejoin Toledo and the rest of the Shadows who were lying in wait to ambush Doña Serena and her companions.

Cortez acknowledged that it was a good plan that the outlaw Moon had suggested. Splitting up the larger force had been a stroke of genius.

Completely oblivious as to the ruse that had been successfully played, Jake shrugged his shoulders. The guy had said it was only a short ride up the canyon. They didn't need his presence to find the robbers. Lassiter bid farewell to Jake, assuring him that they would catch up later in the day, with Crazy Dog Moon and his bunch under arrest. Although it was equally likely the brigands would end up like Turner draping their saddles if any resistance was encountered.

The two men shook hands before each group of riders went their separate ways.

14

Double-Dealing

The Shadows were ensconced within the narrow limits of Laguna Canyon, one hour's ride north of the Penasco Plough fork. Moon had persuaded Toledo to place his men on the far side of the canyon with himself and the Shadow leader opposite. There was a specific reason for this, which brought a crafty grimace to Moon's stubbled features. But he kept that scheming notion to himself, merely claiming that it was a better strategy. Toledo readily agreed.

Charlie Moon's plan counted on Fontelle preferring to push ahead for Albuquerque rather than delay by helping out with a robbery that was none of his concern.

The outlaw was also well aware that the posse would not want the extra help to arrest three outlaws. That would mean a smaller split of the potential reward. With Hardknott Bud Lassiter being renowned for his obstinate refusal to abandon the pursuit of a felon, Moon was confident of being able to split up the group.

He chuckled aloud. The sheriff was going to be spitting feathers when he discovered he had been played for a mug. By then it would be too late for him to do anything about it.

'What amuses you now?' enquired Toledo, who was crouching behind a boulder checking his rifle and revolver.

'Just mighty pleased at how this is panning out,' Moon answered with a positive assurance that appeared to satisfy the Mexican. Toledo turned away, shifting his gaze towards the trail along which their quarry would be approaching. He peered at his pocket watch. In fact, they should be heading into the trap any time now.

Moon gripped his own rifle. He arrowed a chilling glance at the Mexican's back.

If looks could have killed, Manuel de Toledo would have been a dead greaser. The only fly in the ointment regarding Moon's plan was Esteban Cortez. He had never quite seemed to fit the pattern of the obedient lackey like the other saps in this set-up.

How long would it take the critter to return after hoodwinking the posse? He could only hope that his own nefarious scheme would have been concluded long before that.

The telltale sign of rising dust told him that riders had entered the canyon. A bald eagle circled overhead, watching the mysterious antics being played out below. Its broad wingspan caught the gringo's attention. 'A mite too far south for one of you guys,' he murmured. Then a clatter of stones brought his mind back to the task in hand. The eagle was forgotten.

He tensed, waiting to discern how many were in the group. If Lassiter had not taken the bait the plan was dead in the sand. What would happen then was anybody's guess. Toledo was crazy enough to take them all on. Even with a surprise attack, guys like Hardknott Lassiter and Jake Fontelle heading a fired-up posse would be no easy pushover.

Narrowed eyes screwed up tight as the riders came into view.

They were in single file. One . . . two . . . three.

No more. He exhaled a deep sigh of relief. This was going to be easier than stealing candy from a baby. He lifted the rifle. He had given orders that nobody was to open fire before he did. Jake Fontelle was his first target. With him removed from the picture, the rest would be a piece of cake.

After a constriction at the mouth of Laguna Canyon the trail widened out. Buffalo Bob spurred ahead, drawing level with his partner.

'I don't like the look of this,' he grunted. 'Too easy for an ambush if'n those Mex varmints have gotten ahead of us.'

'Yep, Bob,' Jake concurred slowing

his mount to a walk. 'I know just how you feel. Do you think we ought to wait up back at the entrance for Lassiter and his boys to catch up?'

'Makes good sense.'

In his place of concealment Charlie Moon was urging them to carry on into the bowels of the canyon. 'Come on, you dumb clucks,' he growled to himself. 'Only another few yards and I'll have the perfect shot.'

That was when fate took an unexpected hand in the proceedings.

Bob was passing a ledge at shoulder height when a much-feared rattle drilled into his left ear. His horse heard it too. The cayuse reared up on hind legs, veering away from the dreaded sound. The sidewinder scuttered in front of Jake and Serena.

Just at the moment when Moon pulled the trigger.

Bob took the full blast of the .44 Winchester shell in his chest: the bullet that was meant for Jake Fontelle. Before the skinner's body had hit the deck Jake had grabbed Serena out of the saddle and was hurrying them both into cover behind some boulders. Its work of scaring off the potential threat completed, the sidewinder slithered off into the rocks.

All hell then broke loose in Laguna Canyon.

Rifles and revolvers let fly in a blizzard of hot lead. All were aimed at the huddle of rocks where the two survivors lay hidden from view. Chips of rock flew in all directions. But none hit its mark. Jake and his charge hugged the ground. Taken by surprise, at the moment they had no way as yet of fighting back.

As things turned out, however, it was a stand-off. The Shadows had the advantage of manpower, but any move to extricate their quarry would force them out into the open. None of the bushwhackers was ready to put his life at risk.

As time passed Jake found himself a niche from where he could effectively return fire without exposing himself.

Serena could only keep a low profile, trusting that her protector would keep them both safe.

Moon cursed his bad luck. His plan was falling apart at the seams.

It was meant to be Fontelle lying dead out there. He could then easily have dealt with the old jasper and the woman. Now he was faced with a hard-boiled rannie who knew his way around a six-shooter and was more than capable of holding out until Hardknott Lassiter turned up.

Charlie Moon had never personally come up against the tough freighter. But he knew of his reputation. Road agents like Flatiron Bucky Danvers and Dutch Henry had tried to relieve Fontelle of his goods and paid the penalty. Charlie Moon was not about to join them on boot hill.

There had to be a way of turning this disaster to his advantage. While the Shadows on the far side of the canyon continued to fruitlessly waste ammunition, Moon was studying the configuration of the narrow gorge. A chaotic collection of loose boulders filled this central section where they were now effectively trapped. Sure, they could easily retreat to the north end of the canyon. But Moon was determined to secure that headdress for himself. As things stood at the moment, one man could easily hold off a small army from where Fontelle was positioned.

Then he saw it.

A narrow ledge hugged the precipitous eastern face of the canyon. Similar to that on the far side, it ran the length of the canyon before collapsing. But that was behind where Fontelle was waiting. It provided the perfect set-up, allowing him to sneak up behind the critter and get the drop on him.

But first there was the matter of ridding himself of an encumbrance closer to hand. The Shadow leader had his back to the outlaw. He was positioned slightly further down, all his concentration was focused on those who had stolen his precious icon. The other greasers on the far side were similarly occupied. Once Toledo had been removed from the picture these simple peasants would be like headless chickens. With nobody to lead them, chaos would ensue.

Moon swung his pistol towards Toledo. One shot among many, and this obstacle to his objective would be removed. The gun bucked in his hand. Toledo never knew what hit him. He fell forward across a rock.

Assuming the guise of a distraught adherent to the Shadows' cause, Moon called out loud enough for the others to hear. 'The Master has been shot. He is dead. All is lost. Flee for your lives.'

The panic-stricken wail ululated across the hot thermals of the canyon. The demented cry was quickly taken up and passed among the simple devotees of the proposed revolution. Men looked at one another. At first they were unsure how to respond.

It soon became apparent, however, that without their revered leader, the cause of the Shadows movement was lost. The shooting rapidly tailed off as men slowly began to back off up the canyon towards where their horses were tethered.

Charlie Moon's eyes glittered with elation. But he knew that time was of the essence now that alarm and fear had been spread amongst the simple peasantry. Scuttling back to the rock wall, he hauled himself on to the ledge. There he discovered that it slanted down at an angle affording cover which enabled him to make faster progress without being spotted by either faction.

Meanwhile, Jake was puzzled by the sudden cessation of hostilities. He had no idea of the mayhem caused by Buffalo Bob's killer. Only now had it fully sunk in that his partner was dead. It was he who should be lying out there. Unwittingly, the old-timer had saved his life.

From cover Jake's eagle eye probed the loose skeins of gunsmoke, trying to ascertain what was happening. Why had the attack petered out?

Men were flitting between the rocks. But they were moving away. It was as if they had given up the fight. It was a conundrum that was solved moments later when a well-known voice chuckled behind him.

He made to spin round, but Charlie Moon forestalled him.

'Stay right where you are, Fontelle,' he rasped. Serena cried out, clutching at Jake's arm. But Moon ignored her. His whole attention was focused on the dangerous varmint now standing between him and a fortune. 'Throw down that gun and don't try any fancy tricks.'

Jake had no choice but to obey.

'Now hand over the goods.'

The threat of gunplay with Serena in the firing line prevented Jake from making any rash moves to thwart his adversary. He cautiously moved across to his horse where the icon was secreted in his saddle-bag. He removed the magnificent headdress and placed it on the ground, all the while keeping a level eye on the gunman.

But Moon was a wary cuss and gave him no opportunity to turn the tables. A gesture from the outlaw's gun forced Jake and Serena to move away from the glittering treasure. What was meant to be a symbol of revolution and power was merely a means to an end for the avaricious owlhooter. It was going to see Charlie Moon living on Easy Street for a long time to come.

Nonetheless, it still exuded a mesmeric fascination for all who knew of its iconic status, and Charlie Moon was no exception. Greens, reds and blues of precious stones gleamed in the sunlight. It was a once-in-a-lifetime discovery.

But the moment soon passed. Time was passing and Moon needed to quit the scene. This pair of turkeys were now surplus to requirements.

'It's been nice doing business with you, sucker,' the outlaw jeered, picking up the icon and walking over to Jake's horse. 'But there's no way I can leave you here to blow the gaff on my part in this.'

15

Countdown to Destiny

Esteban Cortez had made up his mind. He was going to abandon the Shadows. The power and influence that had been promised to those who supported the movement in a supervisory capacity had initially been a potent enticement. As hacienda foreman he had been one of the first whom Don Toledo had approached. And, as with others, the grandee's eloquent persuasion had easily won him over.

He had later become increasingly disillusioned by the Master's fanatical pursuit of his dream when violent methods began to take precedence over those of verbal debate. The matter had come to a head when Don Alvarez had been targeted. Cortez had greatly respected the aging patriarch of the de

Toledo household. His death came as a bitter blow, especially when the truth of the matter emerged.

Yet still he had hoped that reason and honour would prevail.

That naïve faith had been dashed following the brutal attack on the Salinas Mission.

Cortez had been riding for no more than fifteen minutes when he realized that running away was no answer. He would voice his concern to Don Manuel and trust that wisdom and good judgement would triumph.

He turned round and rode back towards the fork in the trail at the Penasco Plough. The only way to reach Laguna Canyon before the ambush could be launched was to follow a tortuous trail that could be seen snaking up through a cleft in the rock wall. He hoped it would lead him across the top of the plateau to the far side of the canyon.

When he reached the top of the mesa overlooking the field of conflict he heard the steady rattle of protracted gunfire. He cursed his indecision. Then a quizzical frown furrowed his brow. According to that devious gringo, Charlie Moon, they would encounter little opposition from those who had stolen the Aztec icon.

Cortez dismounted and made his way across to the rim of the mesa.

Below he could make out the two factions, engaged in a furious battle. On this side of the canyon he had a grand-stand view of all the action. Then a startling development left him stunned. Murder was being committed right before his eyes.

Moon had deliberately shot Don Manuel in the back. A panic-stricken shout followed. The cry had lifted on the hot thermals. Even though the words were unclear, their effect rapidly brought the shooting to an end.

On the far side of the narrow gorge the men began to pull back. Cortez was nonplussed. What was happening that had caused the peons to abandon their superior position? It must be something the killer had shouted. Then he realized that Moon had planned this skulduggery all along. He wanted the icon for himself.

Now, with their leader dead, the simple followers of the Shadows' cause were like a fishing boat without a rudder. They were unable to think for themselves. Now there was only one man left between Moon and his goal.

The Mexican screwed up his eyes. He saw the dangerous gringo scuttling back across to this side of the canyon wall. But his view was obscured by the overhang. What was clear, however, was that Don Manuel was badly injured, probably dead.

Cortez was in a quandary. What should he do?

The plan proposed by Moon had been a sham. The only way to thwart the blackguard now was for Cortez himself to descend the cliff face and scotch his deadly game. There were numerous cracks in the rock wall. He soon found a steep yet practicable route down through a narrow ravine.

Checking the body of Don Manuel he confirmed that the boss was indeed dead. His body was unmoving, with much blood soaking his clothes, the brutal result of a point-blank and cold-blooded murder. By the time he had followed the ledge recently taken by Moon, it was becoming patently clear what had occurred. Cortez snarled as the full implication of the double-cross struck home.

And now the varmint had the other man and *Señora* Toledo at his mercy.

There was not a moment to lose if he was to save the situation.

On one side of the canyon the two victims stood, silently awaiting their date with destiny. Opposite, Charlie Moon had them covered. A grin wider than a barn door split up the killer's face. And in the middle, hidden behind a boulder, crouched Esteban Cortez.

The outlaw's heavy revolver racked to full cock.

'You ready to meet your Maker?' crowed

Moon. He was thoroughly enjoying the moment of his triumph. 'You better pray that he don't kick up a fuss at you bringing the dame in through them pearly gates, her being a married woman.' Then he appeared to change his mind. An ugly chortle issued from between his lips. 'My mistake, sucker. You'll be OK cos she's recently become a widow.' Moon laughed out loud at his jovial crack.

But the outlaw's sarcastic badinage had given Cortez the time to conceive a plan of action. There was no time to waste. Instantly he acted upon his decision.

Suddenly, a melodic tinkle, low yet penetrating, cut the tense atmosphere. Completely alien amid the harsh surroundings, it stunned Moon, not to mention his two victims. All three turned to face the source of the lyrical cadence. And there, perched on a rock, sat an opened pocket watch.

It glinted menacingly in the harsh sunlight.

A low chuckle accompanied the

tuneful rendition as Cortez emerged from cover. He had shifted his position to come out behind the gunman.

'Slot that hogleg back where it belongs, Moon,' he hissed, jacking the hammer of his own gun to full cock in support of the command. 'And don't think to take me out. There's a gun pointed right at your back.'

Moon's teeth ground in frustration. In the euphoria of the moment he had forgotten all about Cortez. Carefully but with regret he dropped the gun back into its holster.

'Now we play a little game,' Cortez said lightly. 'One way or another the señora will come out of this alive. And she can have the icon to do with as she wills.' Then he turned to address Charlie Moon. 'And you can go free, even if you are a back-shooting coyote.' A humourless smile and a shrug followed as the Mexican added, 'There is only one condition.' He paused, allowing the outlaw to state the obvious.

'And what might that be, greaser?'

The sneering affront did not faze the Mexican. His lurid smile remained constant.

'You must beat this other gringo to the draw. A simple gunfight, *sí?* . . . but to the death.' The smile disappeared.

Serena cried out. 'No, Esteban, you cannot do this. Jake is innocent.'

Cortez shook his head. The steely face was set as though in stone. The machismo of the Mexican culture still prevailed. 'That is how it must be, *señora*. You chose this man above your husband. Now he must win your hand in combat. That is only fair. Do you not agree, *señor?*'

Jake knew that he had no choice in the matter. At least Serena would come out a winner. He shrugged. 'Guess so. How does this game play out?'

'Each of you will have a gun containing one cartridge only,' Cortez explained. 'And you, *señora*, will do the loading, if you please. And do not think to give your paramour any advantage because I as referee have the final say in this.' He raised his own gun to make sure there was no doubting the result of any deception. 'That way, all is fair in love and war, as you Americanos say.'

Keeping a careful watch on both participants in the bizarre contest, Cortez sidled round to where the watch was perched. He handed it to Serena.

'You rewind the watch, *señora*. When you are ready, open it.' He looked at both men. 'You both know what to do when the melody finishes.'

Nervous hands twisted the knurled winder. Serena was loath to complete the task knowing that it could be the end for Lazy Jake Fontelle. She knew now that this man meant more to her than she had realized. But there was no way out. Esteban Cortez was holding all the aces.

Gingerly, she set the watch down.

'Open it, *señora*!'

The brusque command brooked no further delay.

The rhythmic melody heralded the countdown to destiny. With the gun steady to ensure that neither of the participants cheated, Cortez rolled a stogie one-handed and lit up. The blue smoke coiled upwards as though in time to the lilting refrain. His head swayed in time to the music.

Seconds passed, then a minute. Time was running out. Both contenders flexed the muscles of their hands, hunkering down into their preferred stance. Flinty eyes studied every movement as they waited.

'Looks like we'll find out how good that rep of your'n really is,' Moon sneered trying to unsettle his opponent. Jake remained silent, his concentration undiminished.

It was Moon who was the first to display his nervousness first. A single bead of sweat swam down the coarse lines of his hard face.

The music slowed. Cortez dropped his stogie and ground it out under the heel of his boot. The moment of providence was at hand.

Silence. A final reckoning. For a split

second nothing happened. The world and all its happenings ceased to have any meaning.

Then came a blur of movement as both protagonists grabbed for their guns. Each weapon exploded in a single blast. Smoke and flame belched forth. Jake's hat flew into the air. He stood there, rigid, fixed to the spot, arm pointing as twining tendrils dribbled from the barrel of his smoking gun.

Likewise, Charlie Moon. No movement.

But as the smoke dispersed, a red blotch spread rapidly across his chest, soaking into the grey shirt. He staggered. A hand reached for the fatal wound. Shock registered on his twisted features as he staggered back.

His head nodded imperceptibly. 'Now we both . . . know.' The grating words strangled in his throat. Unable to maintain his balance, the outlaw sank to the hard ground. A final hiss sounded as his last breath dispersed in the still air.

The Crazy Dog was dead.

Serena ran across to Jake and hugged

him to her trembling frame. He held her close, smelling the sweet fragrance of her hair. He felt light-headed. His legs felt like they were sinking in mud. Slowly they both sank to the floor.

It was a full five minutes before they were able truly to appreciate that the nightmare was over. That they had come through it safely, and together.

Cortez was the first to make a move.

'I think that it is time for me to leave,' he said as if nothing untoward had occurred. 'It would not do for me to be caught by Sheriff Lassiter. I do not think the Hardknott will appreciate being sent off on a wild-goose chase.'

For the first time, a lazy smile cracked Jake's handsome visage. 'Guess you're right at that,' he agreed. 'What are your plans?'

The hacienda foreman addressed Serena. 'It is for you to decide what is to become of the icon, señora. The Shadows are finished. And perhaps it is as well. Don Manuel sought to overthrow the legitimate government of our country for his own personal gain. That cannot be right.'

The pounding of hoofs could be heard. They were kicking up a heap of dust.

'Sounds like old Bud has heard the gunfire,' Jake observed. 'Time you were splitting the breeze.' He held out a hand. 'Perhaps we will meet down in Mexico.'

'I will look forward to working for Doña Serena when she takes control as head of the Toledo household.' Cortez looked towards the woman. 'If that is all right with you, *señora*?'

'*Sí, sí*, Esteban,' she said, urging the lingering *vaquero* to depart quickly. 'Now go before it is too late.'

With a wave of his sombrero Cortez mounted up and weaved a path through the rocks towards the northern end of Laguna Canyon. Five minutes later he had disappeared among the welter of boulders as Bud Lassiter and his men arrived.

Ever the observant lawdog, Lassiter spotted the body of Crazy Dog Moon and the spreading stain beneath the corpse.

'Seems like some galoot has played me for a sucker,' he growled. The lawman was angry at being duped and was ready to cast the blame far and wide. His gun, along with those of his men, was out and ready to haul off at the slightest excuse. 'You better have a good explanation, fella.'

Jake kept his hand well away from the gun on his hip as he explained the course of events. He was supported at intervals by Serena de Toledo. No mention was made of the part played by Cortez. As far as the lawman would ever know he had disappeared back to Mexico.

The woman suggested that they all settle down over a pot of coffee and some vittles while details were clarified. It was a complicated business.

But first, Jake wanted to deal with the body of his partner. Acknowledging that these people were victims as well as the people of Carrizozo softened the lawman's attitude. He offered to help bury the body of Buffalo Bob. The undertaker, who was a member of the posse, was able to fashion a suitable cross with an appropriate dedication carved thereon.

'What are you folks going to do now?' Lassiter enquired while sipping his coffee and chewing on a tasty tortilla.

'Guess we'll continue to Santa Fe and deliver this headdress to the Mexican authorities up there,' Jake informed him. 'Don't quite know after that.'

'Well I certainly do.' Serena perked up with spirit. She turned to the sheriff. 'We are going back to my hacienda in Mexico.' A sly crease of a smile lit up the exquisite features. 'There is a vacancy for a new *patrón* to help run the place. Perhaps somebody can suggest a suitable applicant?'

All eyes were fastened on to the man sitting beside her. Jake's face reddened. But at that moment he felt like a million dollars.

THE END

We do hope that you have enjoyed reading this large print book.

Did you know that all of our titles are available for purchase?

We publish a wide range of high quality large print books including:
**Romances, Mysteries, Classics
General Fiction
Non Fiction and Westerns**

Special interest titles available in large print are:
**The Little Oxford Dictionary
Music Book, Song Book
Hymn Book, Service Book**

Also available from us courtesy of Oxford University Press:
**Young Readers' Dictionary
(large print edition)
Young Readers' Thesaurus
(large print edition)**

For further information or a free brochure, please contact us at:
**Ulverscroft Large Print Books Ltd.,
The Green, Bradgate Road, Anstey,
Leicester, LE7 7FU, England.
Tel:** (00 44) **0116 236 4325**
Fax: (00 44) **0116 234 0205**

POWDER RIVER

Jack Edwardes

As the State Governor's lawmen spread throughout Wyoming, the days of the bounty hunter are coming to a close. For hired gun Brad Thornton, this spells the end of an era. The men in badges aren't yet everywhere, though, and rancher Moreton Frewen needs immediate action: rustlers are stealing his stock, and Thornton is just the man to make the culprits pay. But these are no run-of-the-mill cattle thieves. The Morgan gang are ruthless killers, prepared to turn their hands to anything from bank robbery to murder . . .

THE HONOUR OF THE BADGE

Scott Connor

US Marshal Stewart Montague was a respected mentor to young Deputy Lincoln Hawk, guiding his first steps as a lawman and impressing upon him the importance of the honour of the badge. Twenty years later, the pair are pursuing a gang of bandits when Montague goes missing, presumed murdered. For six months, Hawk continues the mission alone, without success. But when he stumbles into the gang's hideout, there is a great shock in store. Seems his old companion isn't six feet under after all . . .

RETURN OF THE BANDIT

Roy Patterson

Villainous bounty hunter Hume Crawford is well-known for his brutal slayings: he will do anything to get his hands on those he seeks. Out to find and kill the legendary bandit Zococa, despite reports of the good-natured rogue's death, Crawford proceeds to shoot his way across the Mexican border. But he has attracted the attention of Marshal Hal Gunn and his deputy Toby Jones. As Crawford follows Zococa's trail, there are two Texas star riders on his . . .

THE PHANTOM STRIKES

Walt Keene

The desert terrain was once haunted by the Phantom — a blanched man on a pale-grey horse, who struck in the night and killed without mercy. Wild Bill Hickock shot the legend down once — and twenty years later, when the Phantom's son took up the torch, he did so again . . . With both culprits dead, Hickock and his compadres are satisfied they have laid the ghost to rest. But when a mortally wounded man gasps that the spirit has returned, they must take up arms once more — against the Phantom's second son . . .